Meet Cute

5 Romantic Short Stories

Amanda Hamm

ISBN: 978-0-985065942

The stories in *Meet Cute* are works of fiction. All names, characters, places, events, etc are products of the author's imagination or are used fictitiously.

The Slow Lane

I'm glad it didn't matter in the end because we never decided who followed whom. It certainly wasn't the way I would have expected to get anyone's attention. Of course, I didn't have any idea how I would meet a guy. I thought it was fortunate that I still had lots of time because I seemed to have spent the year since college eliminating the possibility of meeting anyone.

Monday through Friday I was at work. The only available guy in my office was Ryan. Sure, he was sweet and cute but it was not professional to have a crush on your coworker. Saturdays I visited an all-female gym with my friend Shannon. She insisted the absence of distractions made for a better workout. I wasn't sure how much good the workouts did anyway since we always treated ourselves to milkshakes afterwards. But the absence of "distractions" was important to Shannon and fine for her since *she* had a boyfriend. I had already been fixed up with his friends during college so that was another dead end.

Sundays I went to church with my parents. Even if we didn't talk to the same group of old people every week, there was that whole "with my parents" thing. I was reasonably confident that the possibility of meeting a guy did not exist while with my parents.

I didn't spend a lot of time thinking about my lack of prospects. I figured something would change in a few years and then I would meet someone. So the only thing I was thinking about that Thursday afternoon was the clock.

My normal commute was 20 minutes. It swelled to at least 45 minutes while I was stuck on the phone with a customer who seemed to have no idea that the clock was striking 5 and that I was turning into a pumpkin as we spoke. I jealously watched my coworkers file out. Kim gave me a sympathetic wave. Ryan stuck his tongue out at me. He only got away with that because he had been the one stuck past 5 the day before. When I managed to wrap up the call I wrapped myself slowly, for there was no longer any reason to rush, into my cozy fleece jacket. I grabbed my stuff and waved to my boss before heading to my car.

Cars seemed to have appeared out of nowhere to clog my way home. I put on some music as I made that first tricky left. Then I only had to endure the tedium of about four miles of stop and go traffic. I was trying not to think about how hungry I'd be by the time I got home. A good song got my mind off my stomach for a minute. There were two lanes of crawling cars. I caught a man to my right trying to hide the fact that he thought my animated singing was hilarious. I switched off the radio and sat in silence and shame, casting shifty glances to my right to see when I was safely past Mr. It's-So-Funny-to-See-Someone-Enjoying-Herself.

I sighed and watched his car move past me again. I guessed I would have to settle for boredom at least until I could get some distance between me and that smirking guy. Both lanes stopped. I gripped the steering wheel. I looked ahead of smirking guy and noticed my car twin in his lane. Same silver color and same fairly common model. I couldn't see the driver, only his hands on the steering wheel. But the hands were not holding the steering wheel. They were resting against it while playing with some sort of neon pink… thing. Whatever it was had rubbery tentacles that the hands were tugging and letting spring back.

That driver looked as bored as I was. The hands were pulling and snapping in rhythm. I began to think perhaps that other driver wasn't actually bored at all. He seemed to be having fun with the pink tentacles. My lane shifted forward. I watched to my right as I moved up to get a peek at who was in that car.

I expected an old guy. At least someone old enough to have a daughter who left bright pink rubbery things in his car. Since I was only 23 that would have been kind of old. But he turned out to be a guy who looked close to my age and who was attractive enough that I took more than a quick peek. I looked long enough that he glanced in my direction and saw me looking. I quickly focused my attention on the road ahead.

Stupid traffic. His lane moved up a bit as mine stopped again. I recognized that silver car as it pulled up almost level with mine. I could tell he was looking at me and trying to get my attention, but I refused to look over. I'd rather have been caught singing to the radio again than checking out the guy next to me. I turned the music back on. Now I was clearly not ignoring him, just concentrating on something else. My lane moved forward.

Then it stopped. The right lane moved up and the guy stopped just ahead of me. He rolled down his window and stuck his arm out to wave at me. I couldn't pretend not to notice that. I waved back and tried to act like he was the one who should be embarrassed. After all, I was not a grown man playing with a little girl's toy. We continued to leap frog each other and he continued to smile at me each time. There was no ring on the hand that came out the window and no car seat in the back of his car. He seemed available enough that I didn't see the harm in a bit of flirting. The few times I had flirted in the past had ended in miserable humiliation... mine.

I was never going to see traffic guy again so I let myself return his smiles and playfully pretended I couldn't guess that he was trying to get me to roll down my window.

He held up his phone. I nodded as though agreeing that it was a very nice phone. He gave me a look of mock frustration and my empty stomach did a weird twist that wasn't related to lack of food.

Then all of me jumped as a horn blared behind me. I tried to look sorry - honestly it wasn't too difficult - as I moved my car to fill in the void in my lane. Traffic guy looked at me hopefully and used his fingers to flash what I recognized as our area code. My face flushed. This guy might not be hoping to never see me again. I didn't know how I felt about that. I almost wished for boredom again, though only for a second.

Unfortunately, I realized that I had become so not bored that I wasn't paying attention to how far the traffic had moved. I was suddenly aware of being in the wrong lane. I needed to make the next right and I needed someone to let me into the right lane in a hurry. I flipped on my signal as traffic guy returned to my side. I pointed helplessly in front of his car to indicate that I needed to switch lanes. He nodded and offered me the spot with a slight wave of his hand. Awesome. I thought that for once in my life flirting had actually gotten me somewhere.

The traffic was a bit thinner on this new street. It was still slow because of all the stoplights. I wondered if a certain other silver car was going to pull up next to me at the next one and try to work on the rest of that phone number. He stayed behind me though. His turn signal still flashing incessantly to the right.

I flipped my own signal up long enough for two or three flashes and then switched it off. The one behind me kept flashing. He wasn't taking the hint. I had decided that traffic guy must be a moron before I figured out who the real moron was. He was trying to get me to pull over. *I* was the one not getting the hint. Here I was about to obliviously drive right out of his life.

Oh. My. Goodness. Drive out of his life? I cannot believe I imagined that thought in his head. He was just having fun with me, surely. But he had made my commute more fun than it had been in a very long... well, ever. I could pull into that strip mall and chat for five minutes. My stomach rumbled as I flipped my signal on again. Maybe four minutes.

A voice that sounded suspiciously like my mother made me park my car in front of the dry cleaner's. That seemed like a place that would have a lot of witnesses that time of day. I turned the car off and tried to pretend I had ever done something like this before. Traffic guy was getting out of his car two parking spaces to my right. Deep breath in, slowly out.

I opened my door and tried to climb out before I unbuckled my seat belt. So much for pretending I knew what I was doing.

He met me in front of my car. I said, "Hi."

"Hi."

I looked at a dark spot on the sidewalk between us for a moment. "So…"

"So…" he repeated.

My own lack of words was due to an abundance of nerves. I didn't know what kept traffic guy so silent. The grin told me he was more amused than surprised by the situation. I suddenly felt like a 7th grader trying to catch the eye of a senior. I needed to get this over with. Time to rip off the band-aid before my ears got any more red. "Did you want something?" I asked.

"Did *I* want something?"

"Um, yeah… I mean… I assume you wanted me to pull over for a reason."

He let out a soft chuckle. "I didn't want you to think you had followed me for nothing."

"You followed *me*."

He nodded. "After you insisted on my letting you in to turn the same way I was. I thought you intended to lead me here."

6

"Oh, well, I'm just on my way home from work so… nice meeting you." I moved quickly back to the side of my car, aware of how incredibly lame that sounded and more aware of my desire to get away.

"But we didn't meet yet," he said. "I'm Shawn and you are?"

I stopped and sighed, then turned to face him, but kept my hand on the car door handle. "I'm Mia."

"Mia. I can see you're in a hurry, but maybe I could get your number so we can talk more later."

"I… don't really think that's a good idea."

"We were having fun in traffic back there." He jerked his head the direction of that last turn.

I smiled weakly. The part before I had to talk had been fun.

"Enough fun that you wanted to follow me this way."

"I didn't…" I wasn't sure it would be better to explain how I had almost missed my turn because of him. "I'm just not sure I'm comfortable with giving out my number."

"Will you take my number so you can think about it?"

"Um…" I didn't know how to answer because I wasn't sure what I was supposed to be thinking about.

"Here." He stepped toward me and held out his hand. "Let me put my number in your phone and then you'll be able to text me yours if you decide we should talk more."

That seemed like the fastest way back into my car. I pulled my phone out and handed it to Shawn. The look on his face said that he was doing me a favor as he typed into my phone. He handed it back and winked as he turned around. I sat in my car and waited

7

for him to leave first. Now there would be no chance of anyone following anyone. Instead of a last name, he had typed Shawn (call me).

I went home and had a peanut butter and jelly sandwich for dinner. It was easy and familiar, my favorite type of boring.

Kim was the one I talked to most at work. I told her in the morning that I had met a guy but that she'd have to wait until lunch for details. Her eyes got wide for a moment and then she tried to put a serious face over the paperwork on her desk. She didn't ask questions, but flashed knowing smiles at me throughout the morning.

Ryan came back with my lunch just before noon. I packed my lunch the other four days. Ryan picked something up every day and somehow he started grabbing my weekly splurge for me.

"Get it while it's hot, Mia," he called on his way back to the break room. I put down my pen and followed him. The break room was also a conference room, in theory. I had never seen it used as such, but there was a whiteboard next to the microwave and a shiny wood table under the cheesy checkered tablecloth.

Ryan had already laid out my share of the food across from his so I sat facing him. Kim blew in right behind me. She pulled a bag out of the fridge, sat down in something of a huff and said, "Now spill it."

Ryan protectively picked up both of our drinks as though they might be in harm's way. Kim rolled her eyes at him and he put them back down. She focused her attention back on me. "Start at the beginning. Where'd you meet him?"

8

Another employee, Michelle, had come in before I could answer. "Wait for me," she said as she grabbed a clear sandwich box from the fridge. She took the seat next to Ryan and made a show of getting comfortable. "Okay, so you were saying?" Michelle prompted me with raised eyebrows.

"I wasn't really saying anything yet."

"Where'd you meet him?" Kim said again.

"On my way home yesterday." I took a bite of my chicken wrap while Kim's imagination revved up.

"Oh, no! You ran into each other? That's so embarrassing! Wait, at least tell me it was his fault."

My mouth was still full so I shook my head.

"Oh. You hit him!? You must have been mortified. Was he cute? Tell me he was cute."

I was kind of enjoying the spotlight and didn't see the need to rush through my story. Besides, the version in Kim's head sounded more entertaining than reality. I looked at Ryan instead. "This is cold, by the way."

Ryan grinned at me and his dimples popped out. Or in. I guess dimples pop in. But Kim said, "So what! Who cares about your lunch? Tell us what happened."

Michelle didn't say anything. She simply kept me the focal point of her eager gaze.

"Okay," I said. "There was no accident."

"Well, how did you meet him on the way home then? Where else did you go? I've heard you can meet guys over groceries. Did you stop at the store?"

9

"Just let her talk," Ryan interjected.

Kim pretended to zip her lips and lock them with an imaginary key, which she dropped onto the table.

"I better hold on to that," Ryan said as he made a grab for the non-existent key. Kim glared at him as he pretended to stuff it in his pocket. It made me laugh though.

"Here's what happened," I said. "You know I was late getting out of here so High House was a parking lot..." I got three understanding nods and then continued. "I was in the left lane and a guy in the right lane caught me looking at him."

"He was that cute, huh?" Kim asked. "What did he look like? Details!"

Ryan pulled the imaginary key out of his pocket and pretended to examine it. "This thing is broken."

Kim sighed loudly. "I wouldn't have to keep interrupting if she'd tell the story right in the first place." She looked at me. "Just describe him already."

"All right, yeah, he was not a bad looking guy. 20s I think... light brown hair, nice smile..."

"What color were his eyes?"

"I don't know."

"You don't know?"

I shook my head. Michelle also looked a bit surprised that I was missing that detail. Ryan seemed more interested in his French fries.

"I couldn't see his eyes. He was, like, ten feet away in his car."

10

"Okay, so he caught you checking him out…" Kim waved her hand for me to keep talking.

"Looking. He caught me looking in his direction."

"Same thing."

"Not really. I actually noticed him because he was playing with something."

"What?"

"I don't know."

"You don't know?" Kim shook her head in exasperation. "What kind of story is this?"

"One that would go a lot faster if you weren't here," Ryan observed. He bit his lip as though perhaps that came out harsher than he intended.

Kim didn't seem to notice. "So he was playing with something and you don't know what it was. Was he driving, too?"

I nodded. "Yes. He had this thing, something pink and sort of spikey and springy, and he had it on the steering wheel and was springing the tentacles in rhythm. I was trying to figure out what the toy was when he looked over at me. Anyway, we kept passing each other in traffic for a while and there may have been some flirting." I stopped for a moment to take a drink. I thought it might cool off my cheeks.

Kim said, "Then what happened?"

"Well, that's the part that's sort of confusing. I wasn't paying attention and I suddenly realized that I needed to get in the right lane to make my turn. But the guy, his name turned out to be Shawn, had just put on his turn signal and…"

11

Kim interrupted again, "Shawn! How did you find out his name? You had to have stopped at some point. When did you talk to him?"

"I'm getting to that part. So Shawn thought I wanted to turn because he had his signal on and he let me in front of him because he thought I was trying to follow him. That's when he got me to pull over."

"How?!" Kim wanted to know.

"Wait!" Now it was Ryan's turn to interrupt. "You stopped to talk to a complete stranger? You don't think that was a little dangerous?"

Kim looked at Ryan before turning back to me. "Relax, *Mom*, she's obviously okay. How did you know he wanted you to pull over?"

"Well, he left his signal flashing and I realized he was giving me a hint. So I stopped in a well lit and busy parking lot," that part was directed at Ryan who seemed only a little less bothered by my judgment, "and he parked his car nearby. And then we talked only for a minute. He asked for my number, but I wasn't sure that was a good idea. He put his number in my phone so I could think about it."

"Have you thought about it?" Michelle asked.

"I don't think I'm going to call him."

Ryan said, "Good," at the same time that Kim asked me why not. She turned on him.

"What do you mean 'good?' Why shouldn't she call him?"

"She doesn't know anything about him. He could be…"

12

"What? A serial killer?" Kim's tone indicated her derision at the possibility.

"Look," I said. "He just didn't… he seemed kind of arrogant and I don't think he's my type."

"Hang on…" Kim looked suddenly confused. "You stopped to talk to him and you still don't know what color his eyes were? I don't think you were ten feet away in the parking lot."

"Probably not," I conceded. "I suppose I just don't notice eyes."

Kim shook her head. "Well, did he tell you his last name? We should find out more about him before we make any decisions."

"I think she's made her decision," Michelle said. "But it might still be fun to look him up."

I shook my head. "Sorry, guys. I don't know his last name."

"Let me see your phone," Kim insisted.

I handed it over but asked, "Why?"

"We can try one of those reverse phone number look up things. Oh, he wrote 'call me.' That's so sweet." She had already found my admittedly short list of contacts while talking. She was finding a pen to copy down the number when our receptionist poked her head into the room.

"Mia," she said. "There's a call for you. I'm sorry, he said it was really important."

I nodded and she said, "Line 2," before disappearing again.

"You guys aren't going to do anything stupid like call the guy while I'm gone, are you?" I was satisfied when Kim looked scandalized at the suggestion. I already knew Michelle and Ryan wouldn't.

When the customer said his call was important I think the word he was actually looking for was long. It was a good thing I had finished eating before he called because I was on the phone the rest of the lunch hour. I could tell by the looks on Kim and Michelle's faces that they weren't finding any information on Shawn. Ryan brought my phone back to my desk along with my change from lunch. His thoughtful brown eyes seemed to be trying to tell me something as he set it down. I was still on the phone and couldn't ask what it was.

"Yes, sir, I'll look that up right away," I said into the phone. Then I pointed at it and moved my hand like a long-winded puppet. Ryan smiled sympathetically before walking back to his desk.

Kim confirmed later that there was no new information to be had. I wasn't concerned. I had a fun story and that was all I thought I needed from the encounter. I was looking forward to telling it again the next day when I met Shannon at the gym.

We did a class first, something with lots of jumping around and complicated moves that I almost followed. We rode bikes for a while afterwards and I told her about meeting Shawn. She was disappointed that he wasn't nicer so I felt like I told the story well. Then we cleaned up and headed for our milkshake rewards. She had the usual chocolate. I felt like a minor change and ordered strawberry. I had just had my first sip when Shannon said, "Let me see his number."

"What? Why?"

"I don't know. Have you tried looking it up to figure out his last name?"

"Yeah," I pulled the phone out of my bag as I talked, "well, I didn't, but someone at work tried and could only find something that said 'cell phone user.' That's not exactly… oh my goodness!"

"What?!" Shannon asked eagerly while I gaped at the screen of my phone.

"Oh my goodness!" I said again. "There's another new contact here." I put one hand over my mouth and used the other to hold the phone in front of Shannon. Right above where it said 'Shawn (call me)' it now said 'Ryan (call me instead).'

"Is that Ryan from work?" she asked.

"It must be… I don't know when… oh, yeah, he did have my phone for a minute."

"You should call him."

"Really?"

"Oh, come on, you talk about him all the time. You know you want to go out with him."

"But… what if he only meant it as a joke or just to talk or something."

"You talk all the time at work. I think he had to have meant it like you want him to have meant it."

"I don't know."

"There's one way you can find out." She looked pointedly from the phone to me and back again.

"What if I'm chicken?"

"I know you are, but you should still call him."

15

"I'll think about it."

I paced around my apartment for almost an hour after I got home thinking the whole time that Shannon was probably right. I did want to call Ryan. That was why I was clutching my phone the whole time. But I worried that I was also right. Maybe he added his name like that to be funny. Maybe he was regretting adding his number because of what I might think. I needed to give him some sort of out. I decided to text him first. I sent: `This is Mia. Is this a good time to talk?`

I figured he could say he was busy and then that would be that. I would get the hint; he would be off the hook. No awkwardness at work. We could just go back to normal.

That's not what happened. My phone began to buzz in my hand and 'Ryan (call me instead)' flashed on my screen. I swallowed hard to push down my nerves before I answered his call.

"Hi, Ryan."

"Hello."

"So I... I noticed you put your number in my phone." I winced at my lame greeting.

"Just now?" he asked.

"Um, a little while ago."

"How long is a little while?"

I smiled, starting to relax. "I guess it was more like two hours."

"Two hours? Here I am going out on a limb and you leave me hanging two hours after you notice? Did it take that long to decide how to turn me down gently?"

"No... I wasn't sure what you wanted. What do you want?"

16

"Are you busy tonight?"

"You just want to know if I'm busy?"

"Are you?"

"No."

"Want to do something with me? Movie?"

"Okay. You know, I didn't think you were ever going to ask."

"I didn't think you were ever going to call."

My Brother the Match-Maker

Things might have worked out differently if the guy with the dog tattooed on the side of his neck hadn't suggested that I "live a little." It may have actually been a wolf. I'm not sure because I was trying not to look directly at it. Instead I focused on the sandwich I was making for him.

"Yellow mustard or spicy?" I asked.

"Can I have both?"

"Sure thing."

I was grabbing the second bottle when Mark sidled up to me looking for mayo. "So Tabby," he said.

"So Mark," I replied.

"I was thinking it was about time I asked you out again."

"You were, huh?"

"Yeah. It's supposed to be beautiful tomorrow. I'd like to take you for an afternoon picnic. How about it?" He smiled ingratiatingly.

I sighed. Mark and I had worked together at the deli for a little over two years, since I finished college. This obviously wasn't the first time he had asked me out. It wasn't even the first time he had done it in front of customers. I always said no because even though he was very nice I just didn't think things would work out for us.

I glanced at Mark and said, "I'm working tomorrow."

"Susan will let you leave after the rush. We can just go to that park around the corner and you'd be back before anyone here even missed you."

I hesitated, thinking maybe I should just go for it. Taking my lunch hour outside probably didn't even count as a real date. That's when my customer spoke up. He said, "Go on. You should live a little."

"I just don't think it's a good idea." I kept my eyes down as I spoke. My answer was as much for the customer as for Mark, but I was fine if they both thought I was talking to the sandwich.

Mark nodded and turned to his own customer while I wrapped up the sandwich for mine. Now don't think I ignored the guy's advice because of the howling critter on his neck. It wasn't his spikey orange hair or the huge necklace of nuts and bolts either. I simply didn't like anyone to tell me what to do. It might have had something to do with Zach. And it might have had something to do with Kevin. Then again, maybe it was Lucas' fault. Those were my brothers. All of them older than me. There were times when I

20

almost felt as though I had four fathers. The first boy I ever brought home commented on the intimidation factor. I was more concerned with the annoyance factor.

Three might have been an unlucky number for me. I also had three boyfriends in my past. At least one of my brothers had insisted each of those guys wasn't right for me at the time. What did they know? Well, each relationship had lasted between six months and a year and each time the guy had ended it. Yet I still couldn't say I had ever had my heart broken, or even damaged. What I felt had been more like disappointment. I couldn't seem to fall for anyone. Sometimes I wondered if there was something wrong with me. And I wasn't the only one. Word of my latest rejection traveled from Susan, our boss, to Jennifer, who worked with me the following day.

"What is wrong with you?" she asked me while we set up for the coming lunch rush. "I don't understand why you keep turning him down. He's so cute."

"I don't know. But nothing has changed since the last time we had this conversation." I covered the freshly sliced tomatoes and turned to Jennifer, who was my opposite in a lot of ways. She was tall and curvy while I was short and skinny. She had short brown hair and brown eyes. I had long blond hair and blue eyes. We'd only worked together about a year, but it was already clear that our romantic lives could not have been more different either. I was like a lazy river with almost no current and she spun through one guy after another like a hurricane. Always elated at the promise of a new relationship, always crushed within a few weeks. Even when

21

she was the one who decided it wouldn't work she suffered heartache at the disillusionment. She was frowning at me now.

"Well," she said, "I still think sparks would start flying between you two if you'd just agree to spend a little time alone."

"I doubt it. And what if those sparks were only one-sided? I'd hate to make things weird at work."

"You're too cautious, Tabitha. Things weren't weird between me and Dan."

"I think you have a short memory."

Jennifer rolled her eyes. "So we had a little adjustment period. No big deal."

Dan used to work at the deli. He and Jennifer went out twice before he decided they weren't a good match. There had been about two months of tense moments after that, mostly alleviated by his finding a different job.

"Tell her she's too cautious," Jennifer said to the random guy across the counter, who was our only customer at the time and who I still could not believe was included in this discussion on my love life.

But at least he was on my side. He said, "I don't know, maybe she was right to turn him down. Who asks a girl out for a Monday afternoon anyway?"

"A guy with imagination, that's who," Jennifer insisted. "Saturday dinner is so cliché. A Monday afternoon picnic is romantic."

"If you say so. Have a nice day, ladies." The guy turned and made his way out the front door.

22

As soon as he was out of earshot Jennifer said, "Not that I'd say no to a Saturday dinner if that guy had asked."

I only smiled in response. I was not the sort of person who imagined dates with total strangers. My problem was that I could not imagine a date with the one available guy I knew either. Jennifer turned back to the condiment bottles she was filling. The flood of people came crashing through the door soon after.

There were many familiar faces among them. There was the woman who ordered lunch for five or six people each visit. I wondered if she volunteered to aid her coworkers or was simply low on seniority. There was the older woman who always seemed to hunt for the glasses on her head before she put them on to read the posted menu. There was also the guy with the scraggly beard and moustache who always got the tuna salad. I always wondered how (or if) he managed to eat it without spending the rest of the day with tuna salad in his scraggly beard and moustache. And there were new faces mixed in with those I recognized.

Once my line ended, the place got fairly quiet. A majority of our customers took their lunches to go. It was about the time I would have left with Mark and I half expected him to show up and try again to convince me. He didn't so I made myself a simple sandwich and was about to sit in the back with Jennifer when the door chimed.

I turned instead to face a customer I hadn't seen before. For some reason I was sure I would have remembered him. "Hi," he said. He had a friendly expression in his very pale blue eyes and a few days' worth of dark stubble across his chin.

23

"What can I do for you?" I asked.

"Well, I seem to have forgotten my lunch today. What do you recommend?"

"Ginkgo."

"What?" His eyebrows came together in the middle.

"Isn't that supposed to be good for memory?"

He gave me a completely lopsided smile that for some reason made me feel completely lopsided and said, "What do you recommend I eat that isn't still in my refrigerator six miles away?"

I searched my brain for a clever answer and managed only, "I like the turkey and avocado."

"Turkey and avocado..." he repeated the words slowly as though he was figuring out how to pronounce them. He shrugged. "Okay. I'll try that."

Normally when I'm putting a sandwich together I'll verify that the customer wants everything as I put it on. That particular sandwich was enough trouble without adding talking. I couldn't seem to make the avocado slices stay on the bread... I fumbled the lettuce lid... I dropped the bottle of mayo... all while trying to suppress an inexplicable smile.

The guy looked at his wrapped sandwich when I finally got it into his hands. "If this is good, I'll be back." He started to leave and then turned back to me. "Actually, I'm pretty sure I'll be back either way." He flashed another smile without really looking at me and I tried to look absorbed in cleaning up so he couldn't tell how much I liked that smile.

I'd like to say I didn't care one way or another if the guy came back. But here was my problem… I had Tuesday off. Normally, that's not a problem. I enjoyed having a day off. I just kept thinking that this mystery guy who said he'd be back would come back on my day off and I'd miss him. I was still wondering if I'd see him again when I got to work on Wednesday. Mark was already there. He looked up from slicing some meat and said, "Morning, Tabs."

"Morning, Marks," I answered. I guessed we were back to being friends because he was calling me Tabs again. People could call me Tabitha or Tabby. Tabs was not on my list of approved nicknames. I called him Marks for retaliation. He smiled and I was glad to see his eyes return to his work. That slicer had lots of guards and safety features, but it still kind of made me nervous.

I watched Mark while I put on my apron. Jennifer said she was 5'10" and they seemed about the same height from my vantage point of barely over 5 feet. He had dark blonde hair that he kept slightly long and slightly messy. His green eyes were serious and somewhat prone to staring so the unruly hair made him look like someone who had more important things to think about than his appearance. It suited him. I wished Jennifer could be right about the potential between me and Mark. But if I didn't see him as anything more than a friendly coworker after two years, I didn't see how a quiet evening, or afternoon, would change that.

I restocked the cups and checked the levels in the drink machine. Mark finished slicing and came over to where I was chopping vegetables. "You enjoy your day off, Tabs?"

"Yes, Marks. It was fine."

He smiled briefly before he picked up a second knife. He thought it was funny when I called him Marks, which probably meant it wasn't going to make him stop calling me Tabs any time soon. I didn't seem to care as much as I used to anyway. Our staccato chopping made more noise than the soft classical music in the background and we both seemed lost in the rhythm for a while.

"Did you do anything interesting yesterday?" he asked.

"Um, is grocery shopping interesting?"

"Not the way I do it."

I covered the peppers and pulled off my gloves. We were almost ready for the rush. "Did you do anything on *your* day off?" I asked.

"Well, I did not have a picnic… so I did laundry instead."

For a moment I thought he was going to be weird about my refusal and had to shrug off the fleeting tension. "I don't know. Laundry day is pretty exciting at my place."

"Yeah?" He smiled at my sarcasm. "I'm picturing you blaring some rocking music and watching your washing machine put on a show."

"A show?"

"You know, like when it's jumping around."

"Your washing machine jumps around?"

"Hmm… maybe laundry is more interesting at my place after all."

"Hey, guys, we all ready to serve?" Susan poked her head in from the back. She generally focused on paperwork and staying out of the way of her well oiled machine, but was good at appearing to pop in out of nowhere if an extra set of hands were needed.

"I think we got it, boss," Mark said.

She nodded and her office door closed only moments before the front door opened. We had two long lines before long, but we kept them moving.

He was dressed casually again, jeans with a deep blue shirt that highlighted yet contrasted those barely blue eyes. He had dark slightly wavy hair on his forehead and was clean-shaven that day. I didn't realize I had been expecting each person in my line to be him until he was actually standing in front of me. I said, "Hello again."

He nodded a return greeting. "What's your second favorite sandwich?"

"You didn't like the turkey and avocado?"

"I just thought I'd see what else you recommend."

"Because you didn't like the first one?" I had no idea why I was pressing him, other than the excuse to keep talking.

He looked as though he was biting back a smile. "I didn't say that. I'm just curious what else you like."

"What would *you* like me to make for you?"

"I really don't know. Will you please suggest something?"

"Everything here is great. You can't go wrong with whatever you pick." I pointed at the menu over my head.

He glanced at it, then fixed his eyes on me and I felt my face flush. I didn't know what I was doing. There was a smile in his voice as he asked, "Are you refusing to make a suggestion because you think I didn't like your first one?"

27

I shrugged. "I just think a grown man should be able to make a decision on his own. But now that you mention it, you didn't actually say that you liked it."

"And I didn't say that I didn't. Do you give all the customers a hard time or am I just special?"

He unleashed that crooked grin and I wanted to say, "Yes!" I censored that impulse with a slow head shake. "I'm the one who's being difficult? You're in line to place an order and yet you refuse to order something."

"Okay," he said. "I'll order a surprise."

"What do you mean?"

"Make me whatever sandwich you feel like making and that's what I'll take."

"A surprise?" I paused for a moment to give him a chance to change his mind. I also glanced at Mark. Although he was making a sandwich, his eyes were on me. My customer was also looking at me with a hopeful look on his face. I decided to do what he asked. I hoped he liked my idea of a surprise. I wrapped up the sandwich and asked, "Would you like a drink with your turkey and avocado?"

He laughed and also nodded. I handed him a cup and my fingers brushed his for a fleeting moment. Way too fleeting. He was leaving when he mumbled something I'm sure he didn't mean for me to hear. He said, "I think I might want to marry you, Tabby."

I don't know if you've ever had a near stranger talk about marrying you. The impulse is to laugh. Laugh and also take a small step backward just in case he isn't kidding. There was something in

28

his tone that sounded serious, but he was gone and I was distracted by an impatient-looking customer. It wasn't until the place had emptied and I was making myself a sandwich that I realized the truly odd part of what the guy said. He had called me Tabby. He knew my name and I wasn't wearing a nametag. There was no way he should have known my name unless someone else told him.

Had he come in on my day off and asked about me? I was sure he hadn't asked Jennifer. She'd have called me two seconds after it happened with complete details. Susan would have said something. She would not have made a big deal like Jennifer. But she would have said something. That left Mark.

Mark was already looking at me, almost as if he knew I'd been thinking of him. I hesitated though, not sure how to casually ask if anyone had asked about me.

"What's up, Tabs?" he asked.

"Um… did you see that guy today who ordered the ham and Swiss? He wanted me to take off everything but the ham and onions and then add gobs of pickles. It might have been the most disgusting sandwich I've ever made."

"That sounds pretty bad." He paused to enjoy a bite of his lunch. "I thought you were going to ask me if I noticed that guy who was flirting with you."

"What guy?"

"Well, I guess there was more than one. I meant the guy you were giving the most encouragement."

"I was not."

29

Mark snorted and said, "The fact that you know who I'm talking about sort of proves my point."

I worked on my lunch for a moment, not wanting to admit anything else without realizing it.

"Do you know that guy?" Mark asked me.

I shook my head. "As far as I know, he just started coming in this week. Do *you* know him?"

"How would I know him?"

"It's just that he knew my name and I didn't tell him."

"Did he hear someone else call you Tabby? A few regulars know your name."

I tried to remember the customer who had come before him. The specific people I thought of who used my name had not been near him, but I couldn't rule out that possibility. I decided to rule out Mark anyway. "So you definitely didn't tell him?"

Mark let out a short laugh. "You think I'm talking to other guys about you? That's not the case. I'd be the last person to offer advice on how to date you."

I knew he was only teasing me about my unvarying refusals. There was something in his serious eyes that I noticed for the first time though. Something that made me think I might not be simply convenient. I decided to pretend I felt my phone buzz. I pulled it out and found an email from Kevin containing only a web link. If it had been anyone else I'd assume he'd been hacked. But this brother had a habit of sending me unexplained links. If I followed it, I'd likely find a listing for one or more jobs more grown up than working in a deli. I stuffed the phone back into my pocket.

By the time I saw him the third time, I had decided to be bold. The guy mentioned marrying me before he even told me his name. I thought I could probably ask his name and not scare him off. And I was tired of thinking of him as "that cute guy who turns my stomach inside out."

He appeared at the front of my line and immediately said, "What is your *third* favorite sandwich?"

"Are we going to do this again?" I tried to narrow my eyes at him. I suspected that any attempt at annoyance was canceled out by how clearly happy I was to see him.

"No, we are not," he conceded. "I would like to order two sandwiches today. Both salami and cheddar with yellow mustard instead of mayo and no peppers."

"Wow. Are you the same guy? From non-committal to very specific with twice the appetite."

"You can do that for me, right?"

He smiled.

I turned to mush.

Then I remembered my resolve.

"I can. But only if you tell me your name first."

"It's Nathan. And I have to say that I hope I didn't freak you out yesterday when I... well, I was thinking of something from earlier in the day and I really didn't mean to say what I said out loud."

"Something earlier in the day that had to do with me specifically?" I suddenly had a bad feeling.

"Oh! I'm not…" Nathan mashed his mouth closed while his eyes darted back and forth. He looked as though there was something he wanted to tell me and couldn't decide whether or not he should. That's when I noticed that the guy behind him in line had his arms crossed beneath a rather sour expression. I knew I needed to ignore the bad feeling and focus on my job.

There was something familiar about the order I was about to fill. I was reaching for the salami when I was struck with an impulse. Perhaps I should have resisted, but Nathan saw what I was doing and didn't stop me either. In fact, by the time I handed him the sandwiches he appeared thoroughly amused.

"These are both turkey and avocado again, aren't they?" he asked.

I tried to look innocent. "Isn't that what you wanted?"

He laughed. "It's actually perfect. I'm going to enjoy these."

The guy behind him cleared his throat.

Nathan slowly began shifting out of the way as he asked, "Would it be better if I came in sometime when you're not so busy?"

"I think we'd all like that," came a voice from the line.

I told Nathan that I was working tomorrow if he felt like a late lunch and then took the next order. I served the next few customers in record time and they didn't seem to hold a grudge.

When things slowed down, I let myself think about Nathan. I was excited about the chance for a real conversation. I couldn't wait to find out what he had been trying to tell me. It seemed that he had been talking to someone about me. And then I knew.

Zach. My brother the match-maker. I knew it was Zach's doing and I couldn't believe it took me so long to figure it out.

Zach was my oldest brother. He worked nearby and came in occasionally and always ordered salami and cheddar with yellow mustard and no peppers. Zach was proud of the fact that he had introduced our brother Lucas to his wife and was responsible for two other successful pairings. He had decided that he could do the same for me. Twice he had brought coworkers in to meet me. Both of those times it was the coworker who was in the dark regarding his motives. Apparently, Zach was trying a new tactic.

I was cleaning up when I had this insight. I sighed and dried my hands before I pulled my phone out of my pocket and had a quick texted conversation with my brother.

Me: I hope you enjoyed your lunch.

Zach: Did he tell you?

Me: No. I'm a genius.

Zach: Give him a chance anyway. BTW, I hate avocado.

Me: I'll think about it. BTW, if I'd known it was for you I'd have added extra.

Then I stuffed the phone back into my pocket.

"What's up, Tabs?" Mark had just appeared at my side.

I only shook my head. I was still trying to wrap my mind around the new development.

"You look like something's bothering you," Mark pressed gently.

"It's not a big deal." It wasn't. Mostly I wasn't sure that Mark was the right person to hear about it. Then again, he was there and he was asking. "I just found out that the guy who's been coming in here and, as you say, flirting with me… Zach sent him."

"Oh. The brothers are helping again." Mark made quotes with his fingers around the word helping. He understood my problem.

"Yeah, I'm not sure if I want to give Zach the satisfaction of setting me up. I also don't want to be rude to someone who could be a perfectly nice guy just because he happens to be associated with my brother."

"There's another option."

"What's that?"

"You could tell them both that you're already seeing someone."

I was about to say that I didn't think lying would help the situation when I caught Mark's meaning. He was looking intently at me, daring me to see him as my other option. I blushed and looked away.

"I wouldn't ask if I wasn't hoping you'd say yes," he said. His voice was lower than usual, deeper. Then he busied his hands with some packages and returned to his normal self. We were cleaning up after dinner when he brought it up again, mostly in the typical jokey way. "Are you gonna pick me, Tabs?"

"Huh?" A lot of mundane stuff had happened between those two comments so I didn't immediately connect them.

"I just… I don't ask you out to bother you. I'll stop if you tell me to."

I nodded. I think we both noticed that I didn't say anything. I didn't ask him to stop. I had never seriously considered dating Mark because I didn't know *he* was serious. Did I want to date a man who I knew was kind, whose company I enjoyed, who had important values in common with me, and towards whom I couldn't seem to muster the tiniest romantic feelings? Fireworks would fade over time anyway. With the last three guys I had convinced myself that I was starting ahead of the game. It wasn't the same with Mark because we were friends. Could we really change things just by using the word date?

I thought about Mark most of the night, except when I was thinking about Nathan. He was an opposite problem for me. I had never experienced such an intense physical pull towards a man. Nothing else had been close. That felt dangerous when I didn't know anything else about him. I couldn't rule out the possibility that he actually knew how much power he wielded with that naïve-looking crooked smile.

At work the next day I focused on Nathan. It seemed best for both me and Mark if Jennifer only knew of his more casual invitations. I told her everything that Nathan had said, emphasizing the part where he might be coming in to talk to me and ending with my realization. "Then Zach confirmed that he had sent him," I finished.

"So?" she said.

"So my brother should not be meddling."

"Not even if he knew you and Nathan would be good together?"

Jennifer did not understand. She was the oldest in her family and I felt a rush of sympathy for her younger sister. I tried to focus on the problem of how little I knew of Nathan. "What if he actually asks me out?"

"You say yes." Evidently she did not agree that this was a problem either. She could not have squeezed more condescension into her answer.

"Just like that?"

"You like him, right?"

"I don't know him."

"Yeah, but you *like* him." She nodded at me. I was wrong about her limit for condescension.

"That's why I'm having so much trouble figuring out what to do."

Jennifer scrunched up her eyes and shook her head at me. It was as though we were speaking different languages. I knew we wanted the exact same things in a relationship. I wondered if there was any chance we'd both end up with it when we had such different tactics. Jennifer put one hand on each of my shoulders and looked down into my eyes. "Tabby," she said plainly, "stop making this complicated. You like him. If he asks you out, you say yes. It doesn't matter if he happens to know everyone in your family."

"Jennifer," I adopted the same blunt tone and reached up to put my hands on her shoulders as well. "He said he wanted to marry me. There is a chance he is clinically insane."

"He said he might want to. If he had actually proposed, you'd have reason to worry. The fact that he is comfortable with a casual mention only means he has the same end goal. That is a good thing."

"But Zach sent him over here."

"Tell Zach THANK YOU."

She made me laugh the way she enunciated the last two words. I dropped my hands back to my sides as she lowered hers and I felt a pulse from my pocket. "Speak of the devil," I said aloud as I read the text from my brother.

It said: `How about dinner at our place tonight as a peace offering? Lynn is making lasagna.`

I thought it was a good sign that Zach felt he needed to make amends. Maybe he had finally gotten the message that I didn't need his help. I'd have said yes anyway though… his wife makes the best lasagna in the whole world. Even better than my mom, but don't tell her I said that.

Zach replied: `Great! You can come straight from work.`

Jennifer was beaming. "This *is* great. You can pump him for info on Nathan."

"Maybe." I thought about that idea.

"Maybe? Why wouldn't you?"

"Well, I don't want Zach to get the impression he's actually helping. But maybe I can sort of… I could ask what made him think Nathan would be good for me and… hmm, it might be possible for me to get some info without sounding like I care."

37

Jennifer sort of snickered a bit. I wasn't sure what she thought was funny. I didn't ask because I thought I might feel better not knowing. I was already nervous. The feeling intensified as the crowd began to form for the midday meal. I was nervous that Nathan might be in that crowd and nervous that he might not be. And all the while I was disgusted with myself for feeling like a 14-year-old with a crush. It wasn't a feeling I could shake off. (The disgust or the crush.)

I think I managed to get through all the sandwiches without screwing anything up. I know I got through them without anyone complaining and that's almost the same thing.

Jennifer fixed herself something to eat as soon as the place quieted down. I took my time with the clean up, hoping it wasn't obvious that I was being slow on purpose. When the front door chimed, I held my breath as I looked up. When Nathan came through the door, I pretty much forgot how to breathe altogether. I met him at the counter and tried to smile. His was better.

"Hello," he said.

"Hi." I tried to pretend he was just a regular customer. "What can I make for you today?"

"I think we both know what you're going to make for me."

I shrugged innocently. "Maybe if you ask nicely, I'll make you something different."

"How nicely do I have to ask to convince you to make two and eat with me?"

"Are you kidding? She's been waiting for you." Jennifer's voice came from behind me. I wanted to reach back and put my hand

38

over her mouth. I had not been waiting to eat with Nathan. The truth, that I had been too nervous to eat, didn't sound any better. I tried to act casually.

"I haven't had a chance to eat so it'd probably only take one please for me to join you."

"Okay," he said. "Can I have a ham and Swiss and will you please join me?"

I nodded and pulled out some bread and ham. "I'll make you what you what, but I think it's time for you to be honest about something."

Nathan sighed and looked at his hands for a moment. His eyes came back up with a serious expression. "All right. I admit it. I really don't care for avocado."

I let out a short laugh and prayed it didn't sound as much like a snort as I thought it might. I could tell by his face that he knew that wasn't what I wanted him to admit. And suddenly I didn't want him to tell me about Zach. I asked his opinion on onions and had him help me pick the perfect tomato slices for his sandwich. I knew I wasn't really angry with my brother for sending Nathan to me, I was afraid that was the only reason he was there. I worried that once he admitted Zach's involvement, the charade of Nathan actually wanting to see me would be over and he'd stop coming in.

I made the turkey and avocado for myself. Nathan seemed to think that was funny.

"Is that all you ever eat?" he asked.

"No, it is not. I actually haven't had this for a while, but you made me think of it."

Nathan and I sat at a small table near the front window. Jennifer apparently felt she had embarrassed me enough for one day because she made herself scarce. I watched him pick up his sandwich. I guessed he was close to my age. He had kind of long fingers that wrapped around the bread and I noticed a cut on the side of his hand that appeared recent. His eyes closed as he took a bite.

"Better than avocado, huh?" I asked.

He chewed for a moment and nodded at the same time. Then he said, "You're a very good cook."

I let my eyes roll just a bit. "Yeah, I can slap stuff on bread better than anyone."

My stomach flipped a bit at his reaction and I planned to spend the rest of the lunch trying to keep him smiling. We mostly talked about my customers. I had lots of good stories about people ordering weird things or dropping things and there was that guy who had never heard of pastrami. It's entirely possible that I talked way too much. But that was Nathan's fault. If he wanted me to shut up, he should have stopped rewarding me with that smile.

Eventually though, it was obvious to both of us that our time was up.

"I really should get back to work." Nathan stood up slowly and sounded a bit reluctant. I thought those were signs that the lunch had been fun for him, too. I rose equally slowly. It seemed obvious that we were both stalling. It was a perfect opportunity for him to ask me out. I was thinking of lamenting how boring my

40

weekend was going to be with no plans when he said, "I guess I'll see you soon then."

He said it as though there was nothing else to say. He walked out without looking back.

My heart felt heavy enough that it had already dropped below my kneecaps. It'd be on the floor in a moment and that was fine because I apparently wouldn't need it anymore. Jennifer appeared from the back at the sound of the front door. "He said, 'see you soon,'" I told her.

She looked as though she didn't understand why that was bad.

"He had a perfect chance to ask me out and he said, 'see you soon.' That must be his way of saying he's happy to keep flirting over the counter and nothing else."

"But…" Jennifer looked at the ceiling. "This is the same guy who mentioned marriage."

"I guess he realized how crazy that sounded."

"Hmm…" I think Jennifer was as disappointed as I was. But she rallied furiously fast. Her face was all smiles as she said, "Well, 'see you soon' is not 'see you never.' As long as he keeps coming in you have a chance to win him over. Flirt hard on Monday. I bet he'll ask you out by the end of the week." She went back to work as though everything was settled.

Flirt hard? I didn't even know what that meant and I was pretty sure that it wouldn't do me any good to figure it out. I found myself wishing that Mark was working instead of Jennifer. He'd have at least tried to assure me that it was Nathan who was missing out, not made me feel that I'd have a date if I had said or done something different.

Mark was always good at cheering me up. I suddenly wanted to see him and I wondered if that meant something. I decided in that moment that it was worth a chance. First I texted Zach: I'm bringing someone to dinner. Cool with you?

His reply was quick: The more the merrier.

I stepped outside so Jennifer wouldn't hear and called Mark to ask if he had dinner plans. I think he was surprised to hear from me. He agreed though. He met me at Zach's house and was sitting on the front steps when I arrived.

I considered chiding him for not ringing the doorbell without me. If we had been having dinner with *his* relatives I'd have gotten there early and stayed in my car where no one could invite me in, all to make sure we "arrived" together. It was best, therefore, that I did not call the kettle black. I waved as I walked up to him.

"Have you been here long?"

He shook his head and smiled at me somewhat shyly. I didn't think I'd ever seen Mark nervous and it was sweet. "It's nice out here," he commented.

He was definitely right about that. It was far enough into autumn that it was getting dark at 6 o'clock. But it was unusually warm and still in the twilight. I felt as though I was standing in an old black and white photo with Mark looking intently at me as was his habit. The moment was shattered by the porch light flipping on and making both of us squint.

"I wonder if that's a signal that they know we're here," I said as I walked onto the porch. Mark was right behind me as I rang the bell. Zach threw open the door. He was a hugger and pulled me in quickly. His wife was less touchy feely. Her smile was genuinely warm and just as welcoming as Zach's rib-crushing. "I think you guys sort of know Mark from the deli, right?"

There was a brief pause, during which I assumed Zach and Lynn were deciding whether or not they had met Mark. I didn't wait for an answer before I asked another question. "Hey, where are the kids?" They had a five-year-old daughter and a two-year-old son and another boy due in a few months. The way Lynn was rubbing the side of her belly assured me that the third was right where he should be, but there was no sign of the other two.

"They're staying with Mom and Dad tonight." Zach said this with a note of puzzlement in his voice that puzzled me because there was nothing odd about his kids having a sleepover with Grandma and Grandpa. They did that at least once a month. There was something not quite right about the way Zach and Lynn were looking at each other. The four of us stood in the entryway, Mark barely through the door, as the confusion spread.

Lynn regained her composure first. She held a hand out to Mark. "Yes, I've seen you, but it's nice to be formally introduced."

"Thank you for having me," he said as he gave the offered hand a quick shake. "Tabby tells me I'm in for a real treat with your cooking."

Lynn smiled modestly and then gestured to a living room to her right. "Please come sit down. Zach just needs to show Tabby

43

something in the kitchen real quick and then they'll join us." She sent her husband from the room with her eyes. I shrugged at Mark and followed my brother.

When we got to the kitchen, which smelled heavenly by the way, Zach turned to me. He first looked over my shoulder to make sure Mark hadn't missed the oh-so-subtle hint that they wanted me alone. Zach sucked in a breath. "Okay, this is gonna be awkward. Didn't you know Nathan was coming?"

"What!?"

"He's going to be here any minute."

"You invited Nathan?" I hissed. "Before or after I told you I was bringing someone?"

"Before. He was with me when I texted you this morning. I thought you guys talked about it at lunch and that when you told me you were bringing someone that that was your way of saying you were okay with being fixed up without actually saying you were okay with it."

"That doesn't make any sense. How are you looking at me like this is my fault?"

"How could you not know?"

"How could I not know what you didn't tell me?"

Our whispered argument might have gone on a long time except that at that moment the doorbell rang. It was three cheery notes that sent me into a world of panic.

"Breathe," Zach commanded. "This will be fine. A little awkward maybe, but fine. You get out there. I need to set another place at the table." He grabbed my shoulders and spun me around.

I tried to remember his advice about breathing as I made my way back to the living room. Lynn was greeting Nathan. I think there was some sort of introduction between Nathan and Mark. I didn't want to hear it.

Zach joined us shortly after everyone was seated. Lynn leaned over and whispered something in his ear. When he nodded, she announced dinner.

The lasagna was as delicious as expected. I still had difficulty swallowing each bite. It was that awkward. Lynn and I were on one side of the table. Mark was across from me with Nathan next to him and Zach on the end between Nathan and Lynn. For what seemed like a long time, no one said anything that wasn't related directly to the quality of the food. And then no one said anything at all. My head was full of questions that I dared not ask. Did Mark realize that he was an unexpected guest? Did Nathan think I brought Mark to scare him off? Why didn't Nathan tell me that this was what he meant by 'see you soon?' Why was Mark staring at my hands? Why was I more aware of Nathan's presence than anyone else's? Why did my idiot brother think this was the good kind of surprise? I tried to focus on annoyance at Zach. At least that was comfortably familiar.

Zach asked me to pass him the bread. I gave it to him with a look that I hoped conveyed exactly how much he was going to pay for his mistake. He seemed to take it as a sign that he should start talking. He asked Nathan something about work. They chatted back and forth a bit. The tension eased slightly with the sound of voices. I didn't want Mark to feel left out though. I mentioned to

Zach that he was also a Hurricanes fan. This turned out to be exactly the right thing to say. All three of the guys immediately realized that they had common ground relating a recent trade. Since they agreed that the move was totally boneheaded, they were free to spend most of the rest of the meal pleasantly debating which players would have been a better fit to the lineup.

With the guys engaged, Lynn and I were free to discuss some of the cute things her kids had done lately and plans for an upcoming family gathering. Then she asked Zach to clear some dinner plates so she could bring out the dessert. The other guys offered to help and were politely refused. Lynn's dessert was a wonderful mixed berry shortcake, perfect for the unseasonably warm weather. Zach was savoring the last few bites when he noticed that everyone else at the table had put down their forks and were only somewhat covertly watching to see when he would finish. He stuffed the last bit into his mouth. Lynn gave him time to swallow and then suggested we adjourn to the living room.

"Actually," Mark said as we all stood, "if you all will excuse me I think I'll adjourn to my own living room."

"Are you sure? You're welcome to stay longer," Lynn assured him.

"I appreciate that. I just have a few things I'm hoping to get done tonight." He complimented Lynn on the meal again and shook hands with both the guys. Zach pulled him into a quick hug so I think he meant it when he said he was glad to have gotten a chance to talk with him. I offered to walk Mark out because that seemed appropriate. It seemed as though I owed him at least that much.

"You're coming back though, right, Sis?" Zach was looking at me and then his eyes shifted briefly to Nathan in what we all tried to pretend was not the most awkward moment of the whole event.

I glanced at my watch and was shocked to discover that it was barely after seven. I nodded to Zach. "Yeah, I'll come back for a little while." Then I rushed Mark to the door while hoping it didn't feel like I was rushing him to the door. The still warm evening felt less pleasant as we returned to it. We walked slowly in silence until we reached Mark's car. He turned to face me and though I didn't know what he was going to say, I knew it was going to be an uncomfortable conversation.

"So…" he started, "I gather you didn't know Nathan was coming."

"Oh, my goodness, no! If I had known I never would have…"

"Never would have settled for me?"

"What!? I…" I tried to protest, but the horrible squirmy feeling in my gut made me realize that he was right. When Nathan hadn't asked me out, I had called Mark as some sort of consolation date. And I knew that bringing him to Zach's house would get word back to Nathan that he had competition. I didn't know how I could have used such a nice guy in such an awful way. That I hadn't done it on purpose was little comfort. I did the only thing I could. I apologized.

"I'm sorry, Mark. I'm so sorry. I really thought we could try."

47

He sighed for a moment as he closed his eyes. When he opened them, he was staring not at my eyes, but at my mouth. I wondered if he was thinking of kissing me as a final "try" for some sparks between us. A second terrible realization was that I was hoping against a kiss. My eyes filled with hot tears of shame and I worked hard to blink them back. It wasn't fair for me to cry when I was the one who had been cruel.

Mark raised his eyes to mine and gave me a sad smile. "Don't worry, Tabs," he said. "I know you'd never intentionally hurt anyone. We can pretend this night never happened and stay friends."

"You really think you can forgive me enough for that to happen?"

He nodded. "Of course. Now you better get back in there before they think we're out here making out."

"Mark!"

He shrugged innocently. "What? Too awkward?"

I bit back a smile. It was surprisingly not awkward. It felt almost back to normal. He pulled his car keys out of his pocket and started to walk around the car. At the door, he looked back at me. "Just for the record," he asked, "when will it no longer be too soon to joke about the night you had two dates?"

"You said we were going to forget it ever happened."

He waved as he drove off and his smile finally reached his eyes. I walked back to my brother's porch feeling that Mark and I really could be okay. I still had no idea what, if anything, was happening with Nathan though. That had me less than thrilled about reentering the house of awkwardness.

The living room was empty. I stood there momentarily confused until I heard laughter coming from the playroom. Zach's house was weird in that it had a playroom that was completely off limits to kids. It housed an extensive collection of grown up games and a giant LEGO Death Star. I found the others sitting at a table with cards already dealt and a place next to Nathan waiting for me.

"Good news," Zach said as I entered. "Nathan knows how to play Tichu."

I wanted to ask how that was good news. I didn't like Tichu. I typically volunteered to watch the kids so Zach and Lynn could play with my mom and dad or Kevin and his wife or anyone else who wasn't me. Also, Tichu usually took at least two hours to play. I had said I'd come back for "a little while." Apparently Zach figured that since he already owed me for the rest of his life, he might as well get his money's worth.

I sat without saying anything and picked up the cards at my place. A few hands in I concluded that perhaps I had never given the game a fair chance. Listening to Lynn and Zach playfully taunt each other, watching Nathan's expectant expression when it was my turn… I was actually enjoying myself. And I relaxed enough to want to get to the bottom of a few things.

"So guys," I started, "I'm curious why neither of you told me that I wasn't the only one invited to dinner."

Nathan immediately pointed at Zach. "He told me not to tell you, same as when I first came to the deli."

49

"Yeah, let's actually go back to the beginning. You never forgot your lunch, did you?"

"No, I mean, I did." Nathan looked at me as though it was important that I believed him. I hoped that meant he felt a bit guilty for his share in the earlier mix up. I wondered what he thought of me bringing Mark. I wasn't ready to ask that though. I nodded that I was listening and he continued. "If you want to go to the very beginning, that would be about two months ago. That's when Zach first suggested I go down and introduce myself."

"The guy's as stubborn as you are though," Zach interjected, "which only made me more sure it was a good idea."

Nathan ignored that. "Anyway, when I recently found myself in need of a lunch, I decided I might as well check out the deli."

"He tried to be sneaky, but I recognized the wrapper."

"Zach thought it was hilarious when I told him how you made me eat the same sandwich the next time."

"That's not exactly what happened," I said.

"But when I brought it back a third time, with one for him, he was less amused."

Zach made a face to show his disgust at the memory.

Nathan laughed. "I may not be a fan of avocado, but watching Zach try to remove all traces from his sandwich was totally worth eating a few of my own."

Lynn laughed hardest. "You guys want to know a secret?" After receiving three serious nods, she leaned forward a bit and whispered, "There's avocado in my lasagna."

Nathan and I laughed while Zach screamed in mock horror. "Why'd you have to go and ruin it for me?"

Lynn shook her head. "You're as bad as the kids."

"Well," Zach said, "even ruined… your lasagna still beats everyone else's." He moved over and gave his wife a quick kiss. They were very sweet together. For a second I could understand why Zach was eager to arrange the same thing for others. But then I realized that I hadn't gotten an answer to my original question. Although we all seemed to be getting along (and it definitely had a double date vibe), the fact that I had unknowingly brought a date to a date was probably not forgotten. Though I was nervous about probing, I wanted to focus on the part about me not knowing.

"I still don't understand why no one told me the plan for tonight."

"Zach insisted that if either of us told you I'd be here, then you'd refuse to show up. Is that true?" Nathan lifted his eyebrows with a hint of that crooked smile as though daring me to refute the accusation. I couldn't argue with him while he was looking at me like that so I turned on Zach instead.

"I am not as stubborn as you try to make me out. I avoided those other guys because I wasn't interested, not because I was trying to ruin your track record." Zach handed me the cards because it was my turn to deal. The smug look on his face told me that I might have admitted something I wasn't ready to admit. After all, Nathan had told the story of showing up repeatedly at the deli without saying he was interested in anything other than lunch. I kept talking in an attempt to cover. "But you shouldn't underestimate what I might be willing to put up with for avocado lasagna."

Zach smiled as though I had just thanked him for everything. I glared at him while I passed out the cards. It was a good excuse not to look at Nathan until we were safely discussing the game.

By the time Zach and Nathan won, it was nearly 10 o'clock. Lynn had already said how much she was looking forward to the extra bit of sleep with the kids out of the house in the morning so I said we should call it a night. Nathan agreed. We were going to walk out together. I was nervous about being alone with him. Now that I knew Zach had been talking about me to him for two months I felt at a serious disadvantage. Besides, I had only barely gotten to the point where I could be near him without feeling as though my body parts were weirdly disconnected.

I said goodnight to Lynn first and then got another good crushing squeeze from my brother. Before he let go, Zach whispered, "Relax. He likes you."

His words only made me tense up more as I hurried into the darkness where it would be less obvious that I was also blushing. Nathan was next to me on the steps. "Is that your car?" he asked as he motioned to my white sedan. I nodded. There was a black car behind mine that I assumed was Nathan's. "Do you think Zach is watching us through the window?"

"I wouldn't put it past him."

"Maybe, if you don't mind, we could take a quick walk around the block?"

I said, "Okay," while my heart sped up and my legs got a little wobbly. He wanted some degree of privacy. Was I about to have another very uncomfortable conversation?

"That was fun."

"Um, I guess." We both knew that part of the night had not been fun. Zach lived on a quiet street. There was no traffic at night. We were not the only ones enjoying the relative warmth though. A few voices carried from an open window down the street and one of them was a woman with a laugh that was more like a cackle. There was a church on the corner and Nathan suggested we sit on its steps. He hadn't said anything for a few minutes and I didn't want to be the one to crack the silence.

"What's the deal with you and Mark?" he said as we sat down.

"The deal?" No beating around the bush now. I should have been relieved that one of us was being direct. I was still nervous though.

"When I realized he was here with you I figured either Zach was wrong about the two of you being only friends or you brought him as some sort of shield from me. But then you didn't leave with him."

I sat there completely tongue-tied. I didn't want to talk about the way I had used Mark. Honestly, I just wanted Nathan to kiss me so I could be sure he liked me before we talked about anything. My hands were too sweaty to think straight. He could tell that I was struggling with an answer. I'm sure it was difficult to miss.

Nathan took a slow breath. "Look, I'll be honest first. I'd like to see you again and I just want to know if there are any complications before I ask. I'm not looking for details."

I chose my words carefully. "Mark and I are just friends. Well, and coworkers. There was… He was hoping for more, but it's settled now."

"In that case, Zach tells me you like sci-fi movies."

"I do. Sometimes."

"So if I asked you to…"

I was shaking my head a bit and that made Nathan stop talking.

I said, "I think I need to hear a lot more about what Zach has been telling you before I agree to anything."

"Okay," Nathan smiled. "I'm not in a hurry."

"I didn't necessary mean right now."

"Just tell me what you want from me."

What I really wanted was a soft landing because I no longer doubted my ability to fall for someone. But I think my eyes were giving away my more immediate hope, dancing around his face and always landing near his mouth. I forced those traitorous eyes closed so I could focus on finding a topic. Did I want to know if Zach had revealed anything embarrassing or simply check his facts? Before I could decide, I felt Nathan moving much closer to me. I kept my eyes closed as his lips found mine. His kiss intensified and left me with no doubts about whether or not he was only doing Zach a favor. I felt less vulnerable than I had all night. When he pulled away that lopsided grin was back. It reflected exactly how I felt on the inside.

We talked for nearly two hours. Nathan actually did most of the talking. He let me know what he thought he knew about me and tried to even the score with stories and information about himself. He continued to be a regular at the deli while we started dating, but never ordered the turkey and avocado. Zach came with him sometimes. It seemed that Zach and Mark were becoming good friends. But that was only part of it. It turned out that Zach was on a fact-finding mission for his next target. He had someone picked out for Mark by Christmas.

Waiting For the Bus

I am not a creep. I think I should start with that before I talk about waiting for the school bus because I don't want anyone to get the wrong idea about me. I hate that we live in a world where people might get not very funny ideas about a 30-year-old man with no kids looking out his window for a big yellow bus. But that's where we live so I need to state what should be obvious. It really didn't have anything to do with the kids anyway.

I'm a programmer who works from home. That's why I happened to be near my window at 4 o'clock on a weekday. I'm not going to bore you with details about what I do. I don't even talk about work with my coworkers. I meet two guys from the "office" for lunch every Wednesday. Henry is two years younger than me and dating a girl who is still in college, which makes him feel about 10 years younger. Joe is 10 years older and has a wife and 5 kids, which makes him feel about 50 years older. We usually stick to sports.

I live alone in a house that I bought last year. I had planned to wait until I got married so my wife and I could pick out a house together. The low rates after the burst bubble made taking the solo plunge hard to resist. I figured if I ever found a wife, she could still do the decorating. I mentioned this offhand to Joe who rolled his eyes and said I'd end up sleeping on sheets with purple flowers. I'm thinking I could put up with purple flowers if there was a warm body under them with me.

My trouble started on a Friday. I know it was a Friday because that's the day our garbage is picked up. I ate lunch at my desk because I had been focused on a particularly hard to track down bug. When I finally fixed it just before 4 o'clock, I really needed to get away from the desk. I was standing by the window stretching. I could see the trash can by the curb and was thinking about bringing it back into the garage and maybe even walking around the block first. A few minutes of fresh air would be good for me. That's when I saw her.

There was a woman walking down the sidewalk towards my house. Wind was catching her from the side and blowing her long brown hair into her face. Her hands were full because she was pushing a stroller so she kept tossing her head to try to keep the hair back. Then the wind would blow it right back across her face. I didn't think she had any chance of winning the battle. And then she did the most amazing thing. She used her foot to hold the stroller while she bent over and seized her hair for a moment. She

58

stood straight again without missing a beat only now her hair was in a ponytail and I didn't have any idea where the rubber band even came from.

I bet a lot of women with long hair could do a similar trick, but there was something about her movements that… I couldn't look away. It was good that she couldn't see me staring at her through the window like some sort of reprobate. She stopped at the corner to chat with another woman whom I hadn't noticed standing at the corner. I realized they must be waiting for the school bus. The woman with the ponytail must have at least one other kid and must therefore be at least 6 or 7 years off the market.

I still had an even stronger impulse than before to collect that trash can. It was only about 10 feet from where the women were standing. I dashed down the stairs telling myself that there was no harm in looking. I walked casually to the curb. The woman with the ponytail had her back to me. I've always had a thing for long hair and even tied up the wind was having its way with that hair. I nodded to the women as I tipped the trash can back and the other woman waved and said, "Hello, neighbor."

That made her companion turn to greet me, too. She smiled at me. I knew it was my imagination, but it didn't look like the smile of someone who was off the market. It looked like the smile of someone who was still looking.

I tried very hard to make sure I included both women as I said, "You'd think this wind would cool things off a bit." I wasn't just looking now, but talking about the weather was pretty innocent.

"I know, it's still hot!" That was the other woman, the one with short hair. She continued, "97 today, even with the wind. It's like God turned on the heater or something. I'm Anne, by the way. I introduced myself when you first moved in, but you've probably forgotten. You're Wes, right?"

"Yeah. Good memory." I thought about taking a few steps to offer a handshake so that the long-haired woman would feel the need to introduce herself. I was holding a garbage can though. I think keeping your hands to yourself while holding garbage is probably the more polite thing to do.

The other woman told me her name anyway. She said, "I'm Kelly. How long have you lived here?" Her right hand jumped off the stroller handle long enough to point at the house behind me. I knew exactly what my house looked like, but I turned for a moment to follow her finger anyway. She seemed to have some dangerous power over me.

"Almost a year now."

"A year? So we have you to thank for the Christmas decorations in February?"

"Well…" It had technically been February when I got around to putting that away. I know it was February 3rd because I got a letter from the homeowners' association on February 2nd explaining to me the inappropriateness of my display. I decided to hope that Kelly was offering some good-natured ribbing and was not a member of the HOA board. "I think a snowman could arguably be called a *winter* decoration and since February is still winter…"

Kelly's grin widened. "He was wearing a Santa hat."

"All right. You caught me being lazy. I bought that thing because it looked like an easy way to decorate and I knew as soon as I got it out that I'd never be able to put it back in the box so I was a little reluctant to try."

"And how did that work out for you?"

"Let's just say he is in the box. I think he may be standing a little crooked this year, but I did eventually get him in the box."

Both the women laughed. I had kind of forgotten that Anne was standing there with us until I heard her slightly shrill laugh. Then Kelly asked me if I had kids on the bus.

I shook my head.

Before I could say anything else Anne said, "Wes is single. Right?"

I recognized that tone. She mentioned my unmarried status the same way older women at my church said it when they introduced me to their daughters and nieces and others they thought I needed to be fixed up with. She said it to Kelly as though *she* might be glad to know I was unattached and Kelly smiled slightly as though she *was* interested at the same time she glanced uncertainly at the little boy in the stroller, which reminded me that she was unavailable.

I was confused and uncomfortable and still holding a garbage can. But there was a question hanging out there. Anne was still waiting for me to confirm her observation. So I did the only thing I could. I said the dumbest thing any man has ever said to a woman, "Yeah, it's just me and my trash can here," as I patted its lid and started pushing it up the driveway.

The plastic wheels crunched loudly on the cement so I couldn't hear the laughter they must have been stifling. I didn't look back. There was brief quiet moment in between me parking the trash can and the garage door closing when a few words reached my ears. Anne was saying, "…explain who you are."

Like a fool, I latched onto one word. Explain. As in, maybe there was an explanation as to why it might be okay for me to be thinking about the woman I just met as the future mother of my children. I spent the whole weekend embarrassingly obsessed with the possibility of an explanation. By Monday, I had come up with one that I liked.

She was the nanny. She had to be the nanny. It made perfect sense. She was taking care of children to whom she was not biologically connected, but she knew I would assume she was the mom. That had to be why she seemed available and unavailable at the same time. And why a simple explanation would take care of everything.

Monday morning I left the paper on the driveway longer than usual so I could check out the action at the bus stop. Morning bus action was a lot different than afternoon bus action. There were four parents and six kids waiting out there. Several greeted me and I waved the paper neighborly in response. Kelly was not among them. Neither was Anne, but I was less disappointed not to see her.

I was watching for the school bus Monday afternoon. More importantly, I was watching for people who might be coming to meet the bus. The corner was empty. I wondered why the morning had so much more activity. I figured it was one of those things you understood once you became a parent. The corner was still empty when I looked again five minutes later. Kelly was walking toward my house though. She was an attractive woman and I didn't mind looking, but she didn't arrest my attention the same way she had before. She didn't measure up to the fantasy I had playing in my head over the weekend.

My disappointment flashed with the red lights of the yellow bus. It arrived at the corner just before Kelly, and a young boy ran up to meet her. I turned away from the window and tried to focus on my work.

There was a mind-numbing conference call on Tuesday. I say that as though there are conference calls that are not mind-numbing. That was because I was hating on that one more than usual as it dragged closer to 4 o'clock. And I was annoyed with myself for caring that it was nearly 4 o'clock. I heard the bus stop and missed what a coworker was asking me. Now I wasn't the only one hating the conference call.

Perhaps I should have waited until this point in the story to mention that I am not a creep. Wednesday I actually moved a chair over to the window to watch for Kelly and that felt a little creepy. I still hoped maybe she was the nanny. I didn't want to give up on the fantasy, but I knew I needed to give up. I was just going to watch for her one more time so I could check for a wedding ring. Because being a nanny did not automatically make her single. I would confirm the presence of a ring and then get her out of my head once and for all. That was the plan.

She stood on the corner by herself. I mean, there were no other parents there. If she was a parent. She was crouched down to talk to the only other person at the stop, the toddler in her stroller. I couldn't get a good look at her hands. Then she stood up as the bus stopped and her fingers closed around the side of the stroller. There it was. A rock on her left ring finger.

I pulled my chair decisively away from the window. Back to work. Back to normal. Back to not letting my imagination run riot with thoughts of the neighbor.

Thursday I did not watch for the bus. Not at all. I made sure I did not look out the window at any time close to 4 o'clock. I didn't listen when the sound of something loud and probably yellow came through the walls. I was not aware of anything except how much I was not waiting for the bus.

Friday was pretty bad, too. I spent the whole day thinking about garbage. The truck emptied my bin while it was still morning. I could have gone out to collect the bin during my lunch break. I had a few excuses as to why that was not the most convenient time for me to venture to the curb. I kept glancing out to the trash bin during the afternoon trying to decide when really would be the most convenient time to bring it in. It was purely coincidental that I was looking at it again as Kelly was walking in my direction.

Wow.

It must have been really hot outside. There was a lock of hair clinging to her left shoulder, which was left bare by the tank top that fit her exactly the way a tank top should fit a woman. That enchanting aura from the previous Friday was back, even from a

64

distance. I still wasn't planning to go outside. But then she gave a fleeting look to my house. It was as though she was consciously *not* looking at my house and I couldn't resist the possibility that I might have appeared on her radar after all. I was just going to say hello, just going to redeem myself by saying something that did not imply a relationship with my trash can.

I stopped just short of actually touching the trash can. I thought that would make my intention clear without making the smelly bin the focal point.

"Hello again. Kelly, right?"

"Good guess. How are you today?"

I was pretty fabulous at that particular moment. I said, "Good."

"You surviving the heat?"

"Sure, I guess. It helps when you don't have to stand around in it."

Kelly sighed and her eyes sort of nodded. "And I hear the cheese wagon is going to be late today."

I laughed. I hope she didn't think I was laughing at her. "The cheese wagon?"

"Oh." She smiled shyly and looked at the ground for a moment. "Everyone called it the cheese wagon when I was a kid. I think maybe it was a regional thing."

"I must not be from that region because I've never heard that before."

"Really? What did you call the bus?"

"Um, I just called it the bus."

"I see. So you've always had a really good sense of humor."

The teasing tone of her voice and the way she glanced at my trash can gave away her reference to my "joke" about living with aforementioned trash can. "You say the 'cheese wagon' is going to be late?" I asked.

She nodded.

"Can I ask why you're already waiting if you knew it would be late?"

"Oh, I didn't know until I was already on my way to the stop."

I was going to ask how she figured that out while walking half a block, but I think my expression asked the question for me.

Kelly said, "There's a neighbor back that way – I'm not going to point because she's probably watching us out her window right now – who opened her door as I passed to tell me the bus was running late. I get the impression she calls the school every day to find out when the bus left even though it's almost never late. And why would you even call *before* it's late anyway?"

She kind of leaned in while she was telling me about her source of information and I liked the way it felt like she was confiding something in me. Even if it was only neighborhood gossip.

"You're not talking about that woman who was here before, are you? Anne?"

"No, no. Anne's great. She lives across the street." She sort of pointed at a brick front house by tilting her head toward it. "Her kids are tracked out this week."

"Tracked out?"

"It's a year-round school. The kids get three weeks off after each quarter or so, but not all at the same time."

"The kids have different breaks?"

"Yeah, there's a calendar on the website that explains it all if you really care. It's color-coded and everything." Kelly seemed to want to drop the subject. I think she sensed that I was just trying to make small talk.

"Well, I don't even have kids yet so I still have a few years to figure it all out."

"Do you want kids?"

"Um…"

"Wait, don't answer that." I could tell Kelly was embarrassed by the way she pressed her lips together. "That was way personal. I'd like to blame the question on the heat. Yeah, that's a good idea. Let's go back to talking about how it's really hot out here."

She looked away from me for a moment and pulled on the front of her shirt. A different piece of hair stuck to her shoulder as she turned her head back to me. I would have told her that I did hope to have kids. I probably would have told her anything she asked. But I was distracted by her looking so hot. And I mean that in every sense of the word.

Oddly enough, she had a purpose for standing in front of my house and I did not. I thought I should go inside before it became obvious that I wanted to stand around talking to her or awkward that it was obvious that I wanted to stand around talking to her.

"Well, I hope the bus isn't too late. You're welcome to sit on my porch if you want some shade."

She nodded at my offer and sort of waved uncertainly as I turned to grab that pesky trash can. I couldn't tell if the gesture was half-hearted because my offer was so kind and neighborly that she was sad to see me go inside. Or because she now thought I was the creepy guy trying to get the married woman closer to his front door. Either way, as her fingers partially lifted off the stroller handle, the action drew my attention to the fact that there was no ring.

I really didn't know what I was doing. There was no way she'd be interested in me even if she could be interested in me. And yet, there was something that had made her fail to look casually at where I lived and she had taken off her ring.

Now I had a new puzzle to work out over the weekend. Was that the explanation Anne had mentioned? Was Kelly not single, but soon to be single? That was not a better explanation. I preferred the dream where she was the nanny. I wasn't as excited about a newly divorced woman with emotional baggage and permanent ties to an ex through their children.

The thing I really couldn't figure out was why these new (potential) details didn't seem to be making this woman any less appealing. On Monday, I was only pretending not to notice it was almost time for the school bus. I didn't do a better job of convincing myself on Tuesday. Wednesday at my work lunch I mentioned to the guys that I had met a good-looking neighbor. Joe said something about how it was about time I admitted I was old and settled down. Henry launched into a speech about how I had to be careful if she knew where I lived because she might turn out to be some sort of crazy stalker. I didn't tell Joe that I would never be as old as he was and I didn't tell Henry that *I* was the crazy stalker. I just asked if either of them had seen last night's game.

A few hours later I was peering out my window again like the crazy stalker I had become. She was standing at the corner, her usual spot, and I wanted to see if she'd look in my direction. She didn't seem to be looking at the house or pointedly ignoring it either. Her indifference drove me nuts. And not because we had exchanged anything other than small talk. Not because I had given her any reason to wish I'd come out and talk to her. I had given up on rational thought the previous week when I moved a chair to spy on my neighbor.

Kelly waved to the driver as the bus stopped. She waved with her left hand and it was back. The wedding ring. I clearly saw the sparkle in the sun. I didn't know what was going on. Had she taken it off for something innocent, like washing dishes, and just forgotten to put it back on? Did the explanation Anne alluded to have absolutely nothing to do with me? Had I misheard the snippet of conversation in the first place?

I knew it was time I let my ridiculous infatuation die. It had to go quickly and quietly so I could resume my life as a normal person. But it refused to die without a fight. Staying away from the window on Thursday was too intentional to be easy.

Friday I left the trash can at the curb and spent the better part of the day telling myself to go get it. Until about 3:30 when I switched to telling myself to leave it alone. It was a very successful day. I successfully ignored myself all day. Kelly reached the corner about the same time my garage door finished opening.

She smiled at me as I approached and called out, "Hey, us meeting is getting to be a habit. Are you just getting home from work around now or something?"

Her tone was playful. She was either flirting with me or laughing at Mr. Obvious who regularly needed to bond with his trash can when she approached. I knew which one I was hoping for. I seemed to still be ignoring myself.

I said, "I work from home as a matter of fact. I guess I'm just feeling restless by 4 o'clock on a Friday."

"That's great. The working from home I mean. I admire anyone who can tune out the distractions."

"I didn't say I did a good job." That made her laugh. It was only a tiny chuckle so I greedily tried to stretch out the joke for a real laugh. "Yeah, sometimes I mute my microphone during conference calls so I can watch *Clone Wars* while my bosses are talking."

I've never been particularly good at being funny on purpose, but she kept smiling. She said, "My nephew is really into that show... but he's six. He builds lightsabers out of Legos."

Okay, so she was definitely laughing at me now. I didn't really watch *Clone Wars*. I just happened to have seen an episode recently so it popped into my head. Maybe I should have said a grown-up show. "Well," I decided to act as if I didn't care if she thought I was juvenile, "I haven't pretended anything was a lightsaber for at least a year."

I finally got a real laugh and it was worth the sacrifice. She had a nice laugh. She said, "I can't say as much because sometimes Ben wants me to play with him. I actually *have* pretended to wield a lightsaber just in the last few weeks."

"That's awesome." It was awesome. There was something about a beautiful woman swinging a sword - or lightsaber - that was... well, awesome.

Kelly looked at her watch.

"Is the bus late again?"

"No," she turned her eyes to the sidewalk and looked like she was trying not to smile, "actually I must have left the house a little early."

Did that mean what I thought it meant? Was she hoping to run into me again? Perhaps Mr. Obvious wasn't so bad after all. "At least it's a little cooler today. It's kind of nice out here."

"It is," she answered simply. She looked right into my eyes and we had a moment. One of those moments people describe as sparks. It was great.

And then the toddler in the stroller reminded us of his presence by shouting something I couldn't understand. Kelly looked up at the sky and said, "Yes, that is an airplane."

The kid was cute and all, but he was just a bit too much reality for me at the moment. I wished them both a nice day and went to collect my trash can. Kelly said goodbye and that she hoped to run into me the next Friday. I didn't get it. What was so special about Friday? She was at the bus stop five days a week and just assumed I'd wait until trash day? Did I really need an excuse if I was that transparent? Or was this woman playing some kind of sick game with me with the on and off wedding ring and on and off flirting?

71

I ate my dinner over the sink that night. I usually sat at the table and I usually used a plate as well. I was just too restless. I poured the red sauce from the jar over the noodles and ate them out of the pan. I was thinking about how wonderful it would be to have someone else make dinner for me. That's not a sexist thing to say. I'm willing to bet that everyone, man or woman, would rather have someone else do the cooking on occasion. That is why we have restaurants after all. I'd cook for Kelly, too. Yes, I was thinking of Kelly specifically. Not just "someone" else.

I had a disturbing scenario worked out in my head. She wasn't divorcing for mundane "irreconcilable differences." She wasn't bored or looking for a change. She was looking to be rescued by the dashing neighbor. (I was clearly lost in fantasy land at this point.) My first thought had Kelly on the run from an abusive husband. But I couldn't let that happen to any woman, not even in my head, so I turned to a more white collar scenario.

Her husband had been skimming money from a client. I made him an accountant in my head because I liked to imagine him more boring than I was. And I named him Scott. Just because. Kelly of course knew nothing about the embezzlement. Scott was forced to come clean when the client started asking questions. Neither Scott nor the guy he'd been stealing from would involve the police, for different yet strikingly similar reasons, and Kelly was beginning to think the guy could be dangerous. Since she could no longer trust her husband, she would need to turn to her intriguing new acquaintance down the street. She had been sending me signals with the wedding ring. Keeping it on at times so her husband

72

wouldn't know she was ready to escape. I could keep Kelly and her boys hidden until I found a buyer for my house and then...

A buyer for my house? That's great. Even my ludicrous daydreams were anchored by reality. Why was I losing my mind only where she was concerned? It was time to give my "relationship" with Kelly a dose of the real world as well. I was done guessing. It was time to be direct. And there was not going to be any waiting around for Friday. I would simply go out there and say hello. Then I would tell her that I planned to keep meeting her there until she asked me to stop. I was in desperate need of one of those two things: to see her everyday or to be told to go away.

Monday didn't work though. It was one of those days when the bus reached the stop before Kelly did. She turned around as she met up with her son. There was direct and there was literally chasing the woman down the street. Crazy stalker or not, I still had some limits.

Tuesday was my chance. She stopped at the corner and I walked out toward my mailbox. Okay, I planned an excuse just in case I chickened out. There was something different about her. She sort of nodded a greeting. It was very neighborly, very not-terribly-interested-in-the-neighborly.

I was outside though. And I was committed to figuring out what was going on. Starting small, I said, "Any intel on the cheese wagon today?"

She kind of half laughed and half snorted. I thought it was because the bus was pulling up so intel was not necessary. But then she said, "You've been talking to my sister, haven't you? I haven't heard anyone else call it the cheese wagon since we were kids."

She glanced at the bus as kids came pouring out and one of them said, "Hi, Mom."

Then she looked at me and let out a real laugh. "And I've seen that look before. That's the look that says you think you're talking to my sister right now. I'm Elizabeth."

"Oh."

She wished me a nice day and turned toward her house with two kids in tow. I stood there while the bus drove off and then took my mail inside to register the new development. There were two of them. Twins. Either I was enmeshed in a very convoluted plot or I should have seen that coming a mile away. Kelly had said she had a six-year-old nephew. She meant the kid getting off the bus. Everything made sense now. Almost everything. The one thing I couldn't figure out was who was to blame for my confusion. Should I have known they were twins? Maybe I met Elizabeth before and she mentioned a twin sister and I forgot. Or should Kelly have told me they were twins? Surely she's used to people mixing them up. At least I knew why she wanted me to wait for Friday.

I actually missed the sound of the bus going by on Wednesday and didn't think much of it on Thursday. Friday I was sitting on my porch with a book when Kelly walked up with the stroller. I looked at my watch. It was only 3:45. I put the book down and met her at the corner.

"Hi." That was all I said because I didn't know which one of us owed the other an explanation. Or if maybe we didn't owe each other anything.

She said, "Hello. I see I'm not the only one who's early today."

"Perhaps I was more restless than usual this week."

"I think I have time to take the little guy down to that stop sign and back before the bus gets here. If you'd like to join us on a short walk."

"That'd be nice." I fell into step beside her and it was quiet for a few moments except for a faint squeak coming from one of the wheels of the stroller.

She took a deep breath and said, "So I hear you bumped into my sister and I have to ask. Anne did talk to you, right?"

"Anne? The woman from over there?" I gestured at the house where I thought she lived.

Kelly nodded.

I shook my head. "I haven't seen her since that day she was at the bus stop with you."

"I'm sorry. I think. She said she was going to talk to you and I asked her not to but she sounded like I didn't have a choice in the matter so I assumed she did it anyway."

"Um, I'm a little confused."

"Anne thinks she's some sort of match-maker. She insisted that she was going to explain about the woman whose very single sister watches her kids on Friday afternoons. And then you came out and asked if I was Kelly the next Friday so I thought she had had that talk and that you were maybe... I don't know." Kelly turned away and focused on the stroller. I wasn't sure if she was embarrassed or disappointed or both.

"I think I was just making sure I remembered your name right."

"Oh."

"But I was... I mean I am... Would you be willing to meet me somewhere other than the bus stop sometime?"

"Maybe."

"Maybe lunch?"

Kelly smiled slightly and said, "Probably."

"Probably Monday at noon?"

"I like noon. Do you like pizza?"

I nodded and we worked out the rest of the details. Kelly turned out to be just as wonderful in real life as the version in my head. And that's our how we met story. Pretty crazy, huh? Do you know what the most incredible part was though? My future brother-in-law's name was actually Scott. I've never told him that I once pictured him as a criminal.

Now is Good

Emily thought she hid it pretty well. She was a little surprised
when Holly said, "Are you going to talk to him today?"

The whipped cream came to a nice peak on top of her drink
and she swirled around it with her straw. "What do you mean?"
Emily asked in what she hoped was a confused voice. She knew
she failed when Holly laughed.

"Come on! We've been coming here every Friday all summer
just so you can watch him spin the sign out front."

"We come here because I like coffee."

"That isn't coffee. It's a coffee flavored milkshake."

Emily shrugged. "I still like it." Her gaze involuntarily went
over her friend's shoulder, through the plate glass window and to
the sidewalk on the corner where a guy was holding a white sign

shaped like an arrow and waving it in the direction of the coffee shop. "He is cute," she admitted to Holly. "But that's it."

"School starts Monday," Holly said, as though anyone needed the reminder. "If you don't go out there now, you may not get another chance to talk to him."

"I don't need another chance." Emily pulled her straw out of her drink and sucked the whipped cream off the end of it. The truth was that she was dying to try to talk to that guy, but needed Holly to talk her into it. She also needed Holly to believe she talked her into it because Emily wasn't all that interested and not because she was a big, fat chicken. She pushed a dark brown curl behind her ear and said, "I don't need another chance because I don't need to talk to him. He's probably not as nice as he looks anyway."

"As nice as he looks?" The laugh Holly was trying to hide came spilling out of her eyes. "You think he looks like a nice guy based on the way he twirls the sign?"

It sounded ridiculous when Holly said it. Emily did, however, believe she had viewed at least a glimpse of his personality over the summer. He waved when people honked, even when the honker didn't have a sense of friendliness. Once he had stopped to take a phone call and the concern on his face was touching. He laughed at himself when he dropped the sign and sometimes appeared self-conscious when he didn't. He always had a cooler of water and occasionally offered a bottle to someone else who looked hot. And there was just something about the way he held the sign; something that suggested even a simple piece of plastic should be treated with an ounce of respect. Emily was not about to admit any of that, not

78

even to her best friend. Instead she said, "I only meant that good-looking guys can be jerks."

"Only one way to find out," Holly retorted. "As soon as we're done, we're going out there."

"No way."

"Yes way." Holly sounded determined, which was exactly what Emily wanted. She hoped that excited and nervous looked something like resigned and reluctant.

Both girls were shivering slightly after finishing their frozen drinks in the air conditioning so the hot, sticky outside air was at first a relief. Emily only wished her feet didn't feel heavy and awkward. Approaching a stranger was embarrassing enough without doing so on such stiff legs.

Holly was more relaxed. She waved to the guy with the sign when they were still about ten feet away and called out to him, "We thought you looked lonely out here and that we'd come say hello. I'm Holly and this is Emily."

He nodded and held the sign a bit steadier. "Hi. I'm Zane." Zane had thought of plenty of words to describe what he looked like trying to get the attention of passing motorists. Since many of those drivers waved, honked and/or yelled things at him *lonely* had never been one of his words. He therefore assumed that the two pretty girls walking toward him were too nice to call him *pathetic*.

The one who said her name was Holly smiled so that he could see her white teeth all the way back to her molars. She had straight brown hair in a ponytail on top of her head. The other girl had darker brown curls that landed on her shoulders. Holly resumed talking as soon as she had reached the sidewalk. "We both go to Southwest," she gestured between herself and her friend, "and we know you don't, or didn't last year, so we wondered if you were new or go to a different school or maybe you're all done with high school?"

"I'm going to be a senior at Trinity Christian."

"Oh, we're seniors, too," Holly said. "And I think I've heard of your school. Isn't it, like, an all boys school?"

Zane nodded and she gave Emily a look he couldn't interpret. To the girls, the look conveyed the possible lack of competition. It didn't make Emily feel any better about her chances. It seemed that Zane had hardly looked at her so far. This was of course because she hadn't said anything.

Holly said, "It must get awfully hot out here."

"Sometimes," Zane shrugged. Then he pointed with his eyes at the floppy hat on his head. "But the hat keeps the sun out of my eyes and I have water and, well… I don't do any elaborate tricks on the really hot days."

Holly flashed her molars again. "Does that mean you do elaborate tricks when it's cooler? Because I think I'd like to see that."

"Sorry. It's over 95 today so you only get this show." He tipped the sign side to side a bit, which he had been doing more or less all along.

"That's too bad," Holly said. The other girl, Emily, smiled with her lips still pressed together. Her expression got Zane's attention. It seemed to say that she knew Zane never did any tricks, elaborate

80

or otherwise, and that she enjoyed the joke more than she would have a performance. How Zane correctly decoded this look and not the one about there not being much competition is something of a mystery. But the look made him want to include her in the conversation. The only thing he could think of was to offer her his white arrow.

"Do you want to try?" he asked. "I bet you could get more attention with this than I can."

Emily took a step backward and shook her head as though the words "iced coffee" might be poisonous. She even put her hands behind her back. "I, uh… well, I wouldn't want you to lose your job to me when the people inside see how much better I am."

Zane laughed. "I don't think I have anything to worry about. The couple that owns this place is friends with my parents. They thought of me since they only needed someone to do it on Fridays. They have another guy who does this even better than me, if you can believe that, on the other weekdays. I actually work at a movie theater most of the time. And you know what? This is actually my last day anyway since I obviously can't be here during lunch once school starts." This was the point when Zane realized that he was kind of talking a lot. "Also, since you were joking I probably should have just said, 'prove it,' instead of launching into my life story."

Holly nodded. Emily seemed fine with the long-winded answer. "Your school starts Monday then, too?" she asked.

"Tuesday. I guess just the teachers are there Monday getting everything ready." Zane couldn't think of anything else to say right away. That was probably good because he might have said anything else that popped into his head. He waved to the driver of a car that turned into the lot. Then flipped the sign over and back the right way.

"Can I try that?" Holly asked and nodded toward the sign.

Zane held it over his head as though she might try to grab it. He rocked it side to side and teased, "Are you sure you could handle this?"

"You were going to give Emily a turn." Holly put on a playful frown. "Are you saying I look less capable?"

Zane couldn't argue with that. He didn't want to anyway. He hoped letting Holly try the sign would keep the girls around a bit longer. "Okay," he said. "First, there are two very important things you need to keep in mind. One is that this thing is an arrow."

"I can see that. What's the other thing?"

"Well, you want people to go that way." He pointed at the coffee shop. "Do you think you can put those ideas together?"

Holly put a hand on her hip. "I think I can manage." Zane handed over the sign and she said, "You guys better stand back."

Emily tried not to roll her eyes. She normally didn't mind having a friend who liked the spotlight. At the moment though, she was concerned that Zane might forget she was there. She took a few steps back and watched as Holly jumped up and down and showed the white sign to passing cars. One honked. Zane was standing right next to Emily and she wondered what he thought of Holly's antics. Her face flushed a bit as she realized he was casting as many glances back at her. For a moment, she wished he *would*

82

forget she was there. Then she remembered the whole last chance to make an impression on this guy before summer was over thing and began scanning her brain for something to say.

"You, uh," Emily's first word came out as more of a squeak, but it was so quiet that Zane didn't seem to hear. She cleared her throat and tried again. "You mentioned a movie theater as your real job?"

Zane turned to face her. "Yeah, it's totally glamorous. I get to mop floors and everything." He paused just long enough to register Emily's smile in response. "But I might be done with that soon, too. My parents are all school comes first…" he made his voice deep and serious just for those three words, "and they only want me to work one or two nights a week and my boss isn't excited about that. But I'm still in negotiations. I hear there's a pretty heavy workload for seniors and I play in a soccer league that starts soon and takes up kind of a lot of time so it's possible I won't have time for a job anyway. But if I have to quit, I plan to do so without using the words 'you were right' in front of my parents. I think I'd be okay without a job anyway because my grandparents are always trying to pay me to do stuff for them. Of course I'd help out without the money. But they always insist and I guess that makes both of us happy." Zane mashed his lips together and forced himself to look at the car that had just honked at Holly.

He and Emily were quite a pair. One had trouble making herself talk when she was nervous. The other had as much trouble making himself stop talking.

83

Holly stepped back and returned the arrow to Zane and made a production of making sure it was still facing the right way. "Did you see that?" she asked. "Four honks in, like, two minutes. It's a good thing you're not worried about job security."

"Ideally, people would turn in here when they see the sign," Emily said. "Not just honk. Zane might still be better than you."

"Of course *you* would say that." Holly gave Emily a look that made the latter's cheeks slightly pink and gave Zane the impression that at least one of these girls might not think he was pathetic. Before he could fully appreciate that idea, Holly abruptly asked, "So do you have a girlfriend?"

Zane only shook his head. It felt like a good time to not open his mouth and risk elaborating on his answer. All boys school or not, he wasn't sure how damaging it might be for these girls to discover that he was 17 and still completely inexperienced in that department.

"Good," Holly said. "Then maybe you'd be interested in getting together sometime. I mean, with Emily." She motioned to her friend, whose eyes got wide, before continuing. "If you have a phone on you or something to write with, I can give you her number."

Zane slowly pulled his phone out of his pocket and Holly snatched it right out of his hand. She fiddled with it for a minute then handed it back with her molars showing. "Here you go," she said. "We'll let you get back to work now."

Holly spun on the spot to leave and Emily lingered only long enough to offer a shy smile and quick wave. She followed Holly

84

across the parking lot and climbed into the passenger's seat of the small red car. Holly was laughing as she started the engine. "That was great," she squealed. "I think he's going to call you so you better be ready."

Emily was happy about the fact that Zane now had her number. And also slightly horrified. What if it was as difficult to talk to him on the phone as it was in person? Maybe he'd do as much talking and she could mostly listen. That wouldn't be so bad. Holly gave the horn two quick taps as they left the lot and Zane waved the sign in the air in response.

He thought about calling Emily the next day. He thought about it for a few days after that as well. He also discussed it with his friends. They all thought he should go ahead and call her. He was nervous though because he wasn't sure she really intended for him to have the number or if Holly had gotten carried away. He was also nervous because, well, that should be obvious. The longer he waited the more nervous he got and the more nervous he got the longer he waited. He eventually convinced himself that he had waited so long that Emily wouldn't even remember who he was. He kept the number in his contact list and thought about being impulsive a few times during the school year, but he never did.

****

"I'm paying attention," Zane insisted.

"Not to the prof," Jackson whispered. "I'm pretty sure *she* isn't going to be on the final."

"Don't worry. I'm going to talk to her today."

"You've been saying that for weeks. And I'm pretty sure that doesn't make staring okay."

"I'm not staring."

"Dude," Jackson said, "I think she can feel you looking at her."

Zane gave his friend a gentle elbow to the ribs, but then concentrated on the whiteboard for a while in case Jackson was right. He wouldn't want her to have a bad impression before he even got to introduce himself. They'd been in class together an entire semester. It was a giant lecture hall though and very anonymous. He hadn't even figured out her name. She had dark hair that curled down her back and she regularly grabbed a strand during class and twisted it around her finger. She sat several rows ahead and to his right. He had an excellent view of her profile. He had been watching, but not in a weird way, most of the semester and could tell when she smiled at something the professor said. He knew when she was impressed and when she was skeptical. Her reactions always seemed to line up with his and he truly wanted to know her. Today was his last chance. The odds of finding a time to approach her before or after the final were slim.

As the class dismissed, Jackson said, "Good luck, man," as he nodded in the girl's direction. She had a friend who always left class in a hurry while she stayed to pack up more slowly. It was a golden opportunity. Zane nodded and walked up to her before he could change his mind.

"Excuse me," he said.

The girl stopped with the zipper on her bag halfway closed and looked up at him, showing a mildly startled expression. There was also something that looked like recognition in her deep brown eyes. Zane thought perhaps Jackson was right and that she did know him as the guy who'd been staring at her. He figured that was as good a place to start as any.

"You probably can't tell because I sit behind you," he said, "but I've kind of been watching you some in class, and not in a weird way or anything. It's just that you're much better looking than the professor." The professor was a sixty-something-year-old man. "And the way you twirl your hair is kind of distracting. Not that that's your fault. Anyway, I... um, noticed your reaction to some of his more hastily drawn graphs and you seem like someone who appreciates a bit of quality in your supply and demand graphs and I couldn't resist trying to introduce myself. So my name is Zane. Zane Schaller. Will you tell me yours?"

The girl smiled at him uncertainly. It really was Zane. She had noticed him a few times during the semester and convinced herself that her memory was playing tricks on her, that he couldn't possibly be the same guy she used to have a crush on. "I'm Emily," she said. Then she tucked her bottom lip between her teeth while she waited to see if her name registered with him.

"Emily what?"

"Morrow." She couldn't decide if relieved was the appropriate emotion regarding the fact that he didn't seem to have any idea that they'd met before. Relief came anyway.

"I don't know how you're feeling about the final in here, but I don't think it'll be too bad. The stuff he was reviewing today seemed pretty familiar, right?" He gave Emily a moment to nod before continuing. "He's really been a good teacher overall, despite the aforementioned deficiency in the looks department. Sometimes you get a teacher who's really smart, yet somehow never manages to explain anything. My chemistry prof has been a little like that. She has this expression that I think everyone in the class has come to dread. It means that she's done with a topic and we'd better start asking questions or she'll move on while everything is still clear as mud. I think that's the final I'm dreading most because there's a lab involved. I'm just slow at labs. I think maybe I'm too careful or something. The time limit seems to slow me down because I keep checking the time, you know? I know I'd do fine if I had all day. Not that I'd really want to do chemistry all day. That's not your major, is it?" He didn't stop there. A question is usually a good place to stop and the only thought in Zane's head was, *shut up and let her talk.* Yet words seemed to come out of his mouth from nowhere. "I'm working on a Computer Science degree. Some of those classes actually have projects instead of tests for the finals and there's plenty of time to work on those. Or there would be if I procrastinated a little less. It's just too easy to think of other things to do when you're sitting at a computer." Zane's brain was churning *ask a question, ask a question, ask a question* and he popped out with, "So you don't have another class right now, do you?"

He immediately regretted his choice. *Way to hand her an excuse to leave.*

88

Emily shook her head and didn't look disappointed when she said, "No, I have a break right now." She had about an hour before her next class which she normally filled with homework or studying or something else far less fascinating than listening to Zane talk. She couldn't believe how familiar he felt after more than two years. The way he kept shifting his books reminded her of the way he used to handle that sign. The attraction was familiar, too. As was her lack of speech. She was afraid he would leave if she didn't start holding up her end of the conversation. "I'm a CS major, too."

"Really!?" Zane was torn between happiness at finding common ground and concern over the fact that there were a lot more guys in CS classes and that she might have already formed an attachment to one of them. His conflicted emotions had no effect on his mouth. "Have you taken CS 187? I had that last semester and maybe it was just the prof that I had, but it was a complete waste of time. It's called Computer Ethics and I had kind of high hopes. I mean, that's sort of a broad topic and I thought we'd touch on a lot of areas like privacy issues and things that you *could* use computers for and shouldn't or even personal demons that might arise from using technology as a crutch. And most of the class turned out to be one long lecture on how not to be a troll. I swear, if the guy had said 'anonymity is no excuse' one more time… well, I probably wouldn't have been the only person in the class to start banging my head against the desk."

Emily was laughing as though she had taken the same class. Zane also noticed that the room was beginning to fill again. "Uh," he said, "I think maybe another class is going to start in this room."

89

Emily looked around her and nodded. She finished zipping her bag and lifted it onto her shoulder. Zane walked slowly towards the door and Emily stayed next to him. There was red garland around the door, which gave Zane a new topic. He concentrated on letting Emily have this one. "Are you going home for Christmas?" he asked.

"I already live with my parents actually. It's only a half hour commute."

"My parents are close, too. I mean, nearby. Although I guess I am pretty close with them. More so than with my little sister. Although she and I seem to get along better now that we no longer share a wall. She likes her music loud and always when I'm trying to do something else. I got her concert tickets for Christmas, which I know she'll like. I'll probably owe my mom an apology though since she'll have to take her. Bethany is only 15. But maybe they'll have fun. I got my dad a tie this year. Yeah, a tie. He teaches middle school and cheesy ties are his thing. I've never bought him one before because I didn't want to encourage him. Honestly, it could be more embarrassing than it is. He almost pulls it off. But I just couldn't think of anything else this year and then I saw this tie with little light switches all over it and I don't think he has one like that and I really just didn't want to have to go shopping again. I'm sorry, Emily." He turned to her abruptly in the hallway. "I don't know why I can't seem to let you talk."

"I, um, maybe I haven't been trying hard enough."

"So my babbling doesn't make you want to run screaming?"

Emily shook her head and the corners of her mouth turned up in a way that Zane found very encouraging. "In that case," he said. "Maybe you'd be willing to give me your phone number so I can talk your ear off again sometime?" Zane had thought things were going fairly well.

Emily tensed with hesitation at his suggestion though. She let out a slow breath and said, "You wouldn't take my number and then not call, would you?" She didn't ask that because she was holding any kind of grudge. It had just occurred to her that there was a small chance that he might take her number and discover that he already had it. She was stalling to figure out what she should say if that happened.

Zane wasn't sure how to answer her question and yet he answered anyway. "Well, I wouldn't ask if I didn't intend to use it. I guess I can't promise that I won't have some kind of nervous freak out later. But I know I want to talk to you again. If you'll let me."

His eyes were bright with hope and Emily tried to squelch her insecurity, but she wasn't fast enough. Insecurity asked, "So you've *never* taken a phone number you had no intention of using?"

He started to say no and caught himself. "I guess there was one time. I just thought it was the only way to get her to leave me alone." He shuddered slightly at the memory. It had been only about a month since he was approached at the grocery store by a woman who had to have been older than his mother. That just wasn't right. Before he realized what was happening, Emily had turned her back to him and was walking quickly down the hall.

Confusion kept him from chasing her. He thought she wanted honesty. Was the admission of a possible freak out a little too much honesty? Maybe Emily wasn't interested in a guy who couldn't muster a little more confidence. Or maybe she finally got sick of all the talking.

Lack of confidence was exactly Emily's problem. It was what had caused her to walk away in a panic. Now she was having a perfectly unrivaled freak out of her own. And for as much trouble as she had finding words for Zane, she had no problem finding them for herself. She was in a deserted restroom giving herself a lecture as a quiet scream.

"You left?" she hissed at the mirror. "What was that? He didn't mean you. He didn't even remember you. Seriously, what was that!? Way to make him think you're a complete nutcase. If that was the goal, you could not have done a better job."

Two girls entered the restroom and Emily watched their reflections walk behind hers. She had not stopped talking fast enough for Zane to be the only one who thought she was losing her mind. She sighed and left. Giggling came through the door before it completely closed behind her.

Emily found an empty classroom, closed the door, and dialed Holly's number. The two weren't as close now that they went to different schools, but they still talked on occasion and Emily couldn't think of a better person to hear about what had just happened.

"Emily?" Holly's voice came through the phone after only one ring. "What's up?"

92

"Not much. Only I just did the stupidest thing anyone has ever done."

"Oh, this sounds good. I'm glad you called. Wait, was it a guy?"

"Yes! It was a really cute guy who I think was interested in me and I walked away."

"What do you mean you walked away?"

"I mean I turned around and left in the middle of a conversation."

Holly started laughing. This was not the sympathetic response Emily had hoped for. "I'm sorry," Holly said. "I... I'm sure it's not as funny as you just made it sound. Start at the beginning."

"Do you remember..." Emily started to recount the cause of her humiliation. Holly became more understanding and began working to convince Emily that all hope was not lost. She even helped her work out a detailed recovery plan.

Zane did not have a plan. He was going to try to find Emily before their final and let the words fall out of his mouth because he figured that was pretty much what was going to happen regardless of any plan.

She was on the phone. He spotted her from the end of the hall, wearing that pink shirt he liked and clutching a phone to her ear. She'd have to hang up to take the test. Maybe he could at least ask her to wait for him afterwards. Just as he got close enough to hear, Emily said, "Goodbye," into her phone and put it away.

She looked at him. "Hi, um..."

"Zane."

A smile flickered across her face and her voice was breathless as she said, "I haven't forgotten your name. I, um… actually…" She was shifting her weight from one foot to the other and her gaze was moving even faster between Zane and the floor. "The thing is…um, the other day I…"

Zane meant to be patient. He was so relieved to see that she seemed to want to talk to him though. "Look, I'm sorry," he said. "I don't know what I said or did and I even asked… well, I'll admit it. I asked my mom. The only thing she could think was that maybe I jumped the gun on the phone number and I hoped maybe we could just talk some more so you can be more comfortable about… I mean, this isn't stalking, right? I'm in the same class. But I don't want to bother you. Maybe if you'd be willing to wait for me after this final for a little bit. I promise not to be too slow. There's no lab."

He might have kept talking, and "might" is being generous, except that when he paused to take a breath, Emily blurted, "I panicked, okay?"

"What?"

Emily pulled her hand through her hair. "I just sort of panicked about what might happen if I gave you my number."

"You were afraid I might keep you on the phone forever with my constant blathering?" He disparaged himself with such a spectacular smile that she immediately forgot the rest of her plan. And for the record, admitting panic was not part of the plan anyway.

She checked her watch. Only a few minutes to get it over with. Her hand fished in a side pocket of her bag and emerged with her phone. She took a deep breath, not sure how she'd explain if this didn't work, and asked, "What's... what is your number?"

Surprise and bewilderment clouded Zane's expression. He looked happy to be surprised and bewildered and slowly recited the proper digits as Emily typed them into her phone. She held it up to show the screen. He felt his phone vibrate at the same time he realized she was giving him what he asked for. Except that when he pulled out his own phone, it recognized who was calling.

"How did you... Oh!" Zane's phone dropped to the floor. He picked it up and looked from his screen to Emily. "You're the same Emily!? Did you know that? Of course you knew that. I can't believe this. I can't believe... Wow. I guess Zane isn't the most common name. We still only met the one time though. How did you..."

"We only actually talked that one time, but if you want to know the truth... I kinda dragged Holly to the coffee shop a lot of Fridays that summer."

"You did?"

"And not for the coffee."

Zane's hand came up over his mouth to cover the suddenly shy grin this news provoked. He couldn't figure out what to say and for the first time since meeting Emily, either time, his mouth agreed with him. He was even more endearing at a loss for words than full of them. Emily turned into the classroom before Zane could see that her face was turning red. He followed and took his seat next to

Jackson, who nodded his approval. The test was even slower than a lab with the constant distraction of Emily glancing back at him. Zane finished eventually and did not find Emily waiting for him. He did, however, find a text that said simply: `Friday?`

He sat down and typed: `Let me know when you're ready to hear me list all the things we could possibly do together before actually suggesting something.`

Her reply was quick: `Now is good.`

Pizza Heaven

I was looking for someplace that wanted help. That's what I thought I might be able to offer an employer. At 19, I didn't know how to convince a potential employer that I was qualified to do much other than be generally helpful. I hadn't been driving very long when I spotted the kind of sign I was looking for in the window of a place called Pizza Heaven.

I parked and walked toward the front door. My hand stopped just before touching the handle while I tried to draw a few steadying breaths. My nerves were immediately calmed by the wonderful mix of yeast and spices that seemed to be pulling me in to find their source. If I couldn't get a job there, I planned to at least come back for the food.

It was late August and over 90 outside so I expected the typical chilly blast of overly conditioned air when I opened the door. Instead, I was greeted with pleasantly warm air and more of the blissful aroma with upbeat yet still soft music in the background. It might have been the most welcoming restaurant I had ever entered. I know most people are not looking for a meal in the middle of the afternoon, but I was still surprised that the place was deserted. There were three people in sight and I guessed they all worked there by the identical brown shirts with the restaurant logo on the front. I wasn't sure which one I should approach about a job.

Closest to me was a girl about my age who was seated next to a stack of menus. She had curly red hair, lots of freckles and a dreamy expression on her face as she watched two slightly older guys wrestle over what appeared to be the door to the kitchen.

The guy on our side was holding the door closed and yelling, "Not until you admit it!"

I could see the other guy through the window in the door. He said something I couldn't make out while clearly shaking his head and laughing.

"I'm not letting you out."

"Can I help you?"

I turned to the girl who had evidently noticed me standing there. "Yeah, I wanted to ask about the 'help wanted' sign in the window."

"They're looking for a delivery person. Do you have a car?"

I nodded and wondered if the "they" she mentioned were the two somewhat childish guys, one of whom was now chanting, "Say it, Kitchen Master. Say it!"

The girl laughed. "Dave is the chef. Brandon calls him Kitchen Master when they're messing around. They're both great though.

You'd love working here. I'm Amy, by the way. Dave does the interviews, but it looks like you might have to wait for him."

Amy didn't seem to want to interrupt her entertainment. She mostly kept her eyes on the guys while she was talking to me. As though sensing he was needed, Dave gave up his side of the fight and let Brandon fall forward enough that the door opened and Dave escaped. Brandon stumbled a bit and then looked over his shoulder. He nodded at me to indicate that he was going to let the escape slide for my sake. Then he did some exaggerated tip-toeing into the kitchen.

I tried not to laugh at the silliness. I wanted to look like a professional at least until I got the job.

Dave walked up to me looking hopeful. "Hi, you're not here to eat?"

"No, um, I hear you're looking for a delivery driver and I sort of need a job so…"

"Excellent. Come sit with me," he said as he moved toward a nearby booth and motioned for me to follow.

I sat across from him. I had expected an application or something. He didn't have any paperwork though. He just sat and looked at me for a moment.

"You go to State?"

"Yeah, I'm starting my second year."

"Why didn't you work for us last year?" he asked in a very accusing tone, but the sparkle in his eyes gave away how much he was kidding. He had very nice eyes. I had always thought my brown eyes were boring, but his were brown and so completely... not boring.

I tried to focus on the question as if it were a real question. "I worked near my parents' house over the summer and I thought I had enough money saved to last the school year, but I was scrimping a bit near the end so I thought it'd be nice to find a source of income this year. I'm hoping to work only part time." This was a question for him.

He didn't disappoint me. "Perfect. What we need is someone who can deliver pizzas only two or three nights a week. We're closed on Wednesday and deliver between five and ten other days, midnight on Saturdays. Does that work for you?"

"Yes. All my classes are done before five so any day should work."

"Okay, I just realized that I forgot to introduce myself though. I'm Dave Youngblood. You should know that if you make fun of my name, you'll be fired."

I smiled, but I didn't laugh. "I understand. My name is Kara Smith. Smith has its own set of issues."

Dave nodded, then frowned again trying to look serious. I wondered if his eyes were ever serious. "But we're getting ahead of ourselves. I can't fire you if I haven't even hired you yet. Let's get down to business." He put his fingertips together in front of his face and looked over them at me.

I admit I was feeling pretty good about my chances at the time, but I tried to prepare myself for real interview questions.

Dave continued, "Do you have a car?"

"Yes."

"Do you mind if it smells like pizza even on your days off?"

"Oh, I would love it if my car smelled like this place."

"Good answer. Do you have a driver's license?"

"Yes."

"Is it expired or revoked?"

"No." I was biting the inside of my lips to keep from laughing. It didn't have anything to do with his name.

"Can you count well enough to be able to make change for the stingy people who forget they're supposed to tell you to keep it?"

"I hope so. I'm an accounting major."

"That'll work. Can you be gracious to customers who give you a whole dollar for a tip?"

"I can say that Youngblood is an awesome name while keeping a straight face."

Dave laughed and dropped his hands to the table. "Okay, you can work here as long as you're on my team."

"Your *team*?"

"Everyone does it. Brandon - that's the joker who had me trapped in the kitchen when you got here - Brandon started the team thing. He and I are co-owners. When we started he tried to get employees to show their loyalty by saying 'Team Brandon' whenever I walked in the room. But a couple of them would say 'Team Dave' to give him a hard time. It all just sort of devolved into this thing where people say 'Team Dave' or 'Team Brandon' whenever either of us does something worthy of praise or mocking."

"So, like, you drop a pizza on the floor and someone defects to Team Brandon?"

Dave put on a playfully defensive face. "I'd like to say for the record that I have *never* dropped a pizza on the floor, but that's the general idea. Allegiances swing back and forth like that door to the kitchen." Dave smiled to himself for a moment and rolled his eyes back toward the front door. "Except for Amy over there. I've noticed that she's never on my team. I try not to take it personally."

I glanced back at the door and saw Amy absently fiddling with the menus while staring at the door Brandon had disappeared behind. I understood. I didn't find it as amusing as Dave evidently did. I thought it might be all too easy to develop a crush on one or both of these handsome young bosses. Dave's hair was as dark as his eyes and his long lashes drew attention with every blink. Brandon was a little taller with lighter hair. I was looking forward to having him near enough to discover what color his eyes were.

"So anyway," Dave said, "now we're going to pretend that I need Brandon's approval to hire you. I'll send him out to talk to you." Dave stood up and walked quickly into the kitchen.

It took about five minutes for Brandon to come out through the same door. He took Dave's place across from me and eyed me seriously for a time. He inspected his own shoulder when he was done with me. There was what appeared to be a single shred of mozzarella cheese sitting there. I had a feeling that he had put it there just so he could flick it off as he did before he drew an exaggerated breath. Then he finally opened his mouth.

"Would you be willing to break the speed limit to deliver our pizzas in a timely manner?"

That sounded like a trick question so I asked, "Is that a trick question?"

He broke into a broad grin. "You pass just by recognizing a trick question. Of course we would never condone speeding." He winked. "Dave told me he thought he was too easy on you and that I should ask some hard questions. He knows I'm no good at interviews anyway though so... oh!" Brandon stopped abruptly and cast a shifty glance back toward the door to the kitchen. Then he leaned closer to my side of the table. I felt another bit of sympathy for Amy as his pale blue eyes met mine. "Would you be willing to help me get him?"

"Get him?"

"Yeah. Don't worry. He likes it when I play tricks on him."

"He likes it? I don't think I believe that."

"Okay, possibly I'm exaggerating. But it'll be great."

"What do you want me to do?"

"Just pretend the interview is going badly. Like maybe put your head down as if I made you cry. Dave hates crying. He'll be totally freaked out."

"So you'll hire me for sure if I help you get him?"

"Absolutely. Can you maybe make fake crying noises or something?"

"I can really cry, actually." It wasn't a skill I got to show off very often. I closed my eyes and thought of them getting watery.

"You can cry at will?"

I nodded and opened my eyes. The first tear dripped out of the corner of one eye.

Brandon was looking at me with extreme reverence. He said, "That is the scariest superpower I have ever seen."

A short laugh escaped as I lost my focus. "I can't do it if you make me laugh."

"Sorry."

I looked at the table and felt a few more tears forming, just in time. Dave opened the kitchen door.

Brandon launched into a hurried apology for something he hadn't said. "I'm sorry, okay? Pretend I didn't say that. Dave should never have me do interviews." He was very convincing. Dave walked right up to us and nudged Brandon on the arm.

"What did you do?" he hissed.

I glanced up and he looked so stricken that I couldn't keep up the gag. I pointed at Brandon. "He made me do it."

"And you were awesome." Brandon held up his hand for me to slap.

Dave stared at us in disbelief for a moment. Finally he shook his head and said, "So much for being on my team."

Brandon stood up. "Dude, she can cry on purpose. How could I not use that?"

Dave sighed and looked at me warily. "I'm going to remember this when you ask for a night off because someone you know died."

I tried to look remorseful, but I don't think it worked. Dave was taking it too well. He handed me two T-shirts like the ones they were wearing. "This is your uniform," he said. "You can wear

104

whatever you want with it and let me apologize in advance for any rude comments you may receive while wearing it. Brandon designed the shirts."

"Hey, it's not my fault some guys can't keep their minds on the pizza." Brandon looked at me when he was finished defending himself. "Can you start Thursday?"

"Sure," I said. It was Monday. I wished he had asked about Tuesday.

Brandon waved and said he'd see me on Thursday before he turned back toward the kitchen. The back of his shirt said, "Enjoy!" and I suddenly realized why some girls would not be thinking about pizza either. Dave also handed me some paperwork to fill out and bring back. I thanked him and took everything to my car.

That Thursday I got my first peek at where the magic happened. Brandon greeted me at the door and led me into the kitchen. Dave was standing over a big pot of sauce and some guy I didn't know was filling a vat with shredded cheese. Brandon made them part of the tour. "This is where we make the goods. That's Josh. Don't talk to him though. He can't do two things at once. That's the oven. It's hot. Those are boxes. Folding boxes is a good way to keep busy if you ever find yourself waiting for something to deliver. You already know Dave." Dave gave me a sort of half salute as a greeting as we walked past. Brandon continued to show me where to find the orders ready to go out and where to put receipts and change. He pointed out the office and told me that "underlings" were not allowed in there. I didn't know if he was kidding. He also told me that I wouldn't want to go in there anyway because it was very boring. *That* I believed.

"And here's something very important," Brandon was saying as he pointed to half a pizza on a corner table. "This is where Dave puts the pizzas we're allowed to eat. Sometimes he makes one just for us, but usually we eat the mistakes."

"We don't make mistakes here," Dave cut in.

"Right." Brandon nodded. "I mean the pizzas the customers forgot to order the way they wanted. And this," Brandon picked up something flat with a logo that matched the shirts, "is a very cool magnet to put on your car when you're making deliveries." He put it back down. "But you'll just be riding with Lance today."

Dave looked up suddenly. "Hey, where *is* Lance?"

"I sent him on an errand."

Dave rolled his eyes. "Please tell me he's not returning another library book for you."

"Don't worry," Brandon answered. "It's a very important errand."

Dave shook his head. He may have had more to say on the subject, but reached for the ringing phone instead.

Brandon rubbed his hands together. "Ah, the evening rush begins."

I stood back and watched as Dave and Josh began putting together some pizzas. Brandon answered another call while they worked. Pizzas were in the oven when a very tall skinny guy came in the back door. I assumed that was Lance. He handed Brandon a plastic shopping bag and grabbed a slice from that corner table. He closed his eyes as he took a bite. Then he sighed as he chewed. He said, "Team Dave. This is the best pizza I've had since... When was my last shift? Tuesday. Best pizza since Tuesday."

"Eat it fast," Dave said. "We'll need you for real work in a minute. And you're taking Kara." He tilted his head in my direction and Lance seemed to notice me for the first time. His eyes got wider and I wondered if that was how he took in all new people.

Lance nodded slowly. "Well, I'm Lance and he just said you're Kara so I guess that makes us introduced. I'd shake your hand except that I'm eating and I'm thinking you wouldn't find the grease polite."

"That's okay. It's still nice to meet you." I tried to smile, but felt a bit awkward under his scrutiny. There was nothing remotely threatening about his gaze. It was simply intense.

A few minutes later I was climbing into a small sedan with Lance, something he did with surprising ease considering that he seemed to me to be all legs. As he pulled out of the parking lot he said, "We'll alternate deliveries so you can watch and practice and... so there's two ways we can handle the tips."

"Oh, no. I'm just tagging along. You can..." I felt a sudden panic. I didn't want to alienate my new coworker by stealing half his tips.

Lance shook his head and otherwise kept talking as though I hadn't interrupted. "We can share one of two ways. Either we claim the tips given at the doors we each visit or we pool them throughout the night and go fifty-fifty at the end of it."

"Fifty-fifty is fine, but you really…"

"Before you agree to anything, you should know that pretty girls tend to get better tips."

I muttered something about how I didn't think that would help me. I wasn't trying to insult myself. I thought I was at least average looking, but was mostly thinking about what I considered an unflattering T-shirt. And my shiny almost black hair was in a basic ponytail. Lance looked over at me only for a second. He was driving after all. I read a lot in that second though. He wasn't as attractive as either of my new bosses, but he had the most expressive eyes I had ever seen and they were amazing. That one look told me that he thought I was pretty and that he was disappointed that his attempt at a compliment seemed to have missed the mark.

I didn't say anything for a while. I'm not sure Lance even noticed. He just kept jabbering on. "I'm sorry my car isn't bigger so you'd be more comfortable. You'll love working for Brandon and Dave though. Everyone does. They've been friends pretty much since they were babies. Brandon's parents died in a car accident when they were in college. He and an older sister split the inheritance and insurance money. I don't know how much it was. That's not my business really. But I guess it was enough to start the restaurant right away. They had talked about going into business together after college anyway and then… See that house right there? Last year they had an awesome Halloween display with lights and giant moving spiders and everything. I wonder if they'll do that again. Anyway, Brandon and Dave opened only a few months after

108

they graduated. I was one of their first hires. That's why I get the honor of training." He smiled as though he was kidding. I think he may have actually felt honored though. "Okay, here we are."

Lance grabbed the two pizzas we were delivering and I hung back a bit to watch and stay out of the way. "I think this house used to be white," he said.

It did have the look of a freshly painted house. I didn't really need to know it might have been a different color. Lance seemed to say just about every thought that came into his head. I didn't mind. I didn't mind because it seemed to be me. Something about me was making him very nervous and I found that flattering.

I missed his company my next night. I was given Lance's number as well as the restaurant phone just in case and set loose on my own. I think I did fine. I passed Lance in the parking lot a few times and he told me how glad he was to see me each time. After about two weeks, he finished his last delivery a few minutes ahead of me and waited so we could walk out together.

"Did you have a good night?" he asked.

"Not bad. You?"

"A little weird actually. I went to the same house twice and was afraid maybe we made a mistake, but it turned out that two different people placed orders without talking to each other. Um, Kara?"

"Yeah?" I turned to give him my attention because I thought I knew what he was going to ask.

"I noticed neither one of us is on the schedule for tomorrow and I hoped maybe you'd be willing to see a movie with me. Please?"

I predicted correctly except without the odd please. He made me feel like the most beautiful girl in the world when he looked at me so he could ask any way he wanted. I said yes. One date turned into two and then three. It was intoxicating to be with someone who could inflate my ego with a glance. So much so that it took about six months for me to admit to myself that we wouldn't work as a couple. It was even harder to admit that to Lance. He cried and I cried because I was responsible.

The only consolation was that my bosses were great about the whole embarrassing situation. They made sure to schedule the two of us on opposite nights afterwards. Lance graduated two months later and moved on to a full time job in his field. He moved to a different city as well.

I asked if I could go home to my parents for the summer and still have a job when I got back in the fall. Brandon said they didn't think they could go on without me. It was a corny line. I was grateful for it. I probably would have tried to commute the two hours if I had to. The job was that great because the people were that great. Brandon and Dave were like the older brothers I didn't have and they really knew how to put together a team. We always felt like a team regardless of whether that happened to be Team Brandon or Team Dave at any particular moment.

It felt like home coming back in the fall and the first few months flew by. One evening I was the last to come back for the

110

night. I found Dave in the office. He looked like he was doing some paperwork, but I knew he was actually waiting for me and not wanting me to think he was waiting on me. "I'm done. Should we call it a night?"

He looked up and smiled at me. "Yeah, I guess so." He stretched and stood up.

"Brandon's better today, right?" I asked. He had called in sick the day before, but generally had Fridays off anyway.

"Yeah, he's okay." Dave smiled to himself. "Actually I suspect he's better than okay. He had a date tonight."

"Really? Good for him."

"Would you say the same if it was me?"

I thought that was a weird question. "Of course."

Dave looked wistful for a moment. He seemed to be in a strange mood. "Actually, can you sit for just a minute? I wanted to ask you something."

He gestured to a chair near the one he was still standing in front of. I was a bit surprised because I had still never actually set foot in the office. I walked in slowly. "I thought peons weren't allowed in the inner sanctuary."

"Honestly? We try to keep new people out until we trust them. I trust you."

A serious answer? Now I was worried that something was up. I took the chair anyway.

"Well, you know Wendy is leaving us and I was wondering if you'd be interested in switching to work in the dining room. It'd

111

mean more hours, some during the day. Less wear on your car though."

"I think I'd really like that. Actually, I was thinking about renting an apartment next year instead of staying in the dorms and I'd need more cash flow for that. It wouldn't be a bad idea to get a head start."

"Were you thinking of leaving us?" Dave gaped at me.

"Never. I figured if I needed more money and couldn't get it here I'd find a second job that worked around this one. I don't know if I could have actually done that, but that would have been the dream."

"The dream?"

"Yes. I'm never leaving here. When I have to find a 'real' job after school, I'll just come here for all my meals."

"You'd miss the food that much, huh?" He sounded disappointed, which was odd since he made the food we were talking about.

"Not just the food," I assured him.

"Okay, so you're on tomorrow. Can you drive one more time and then work 4 – 10 on Tuesday in the dining room? Amy can train you."

"Perfect."

Dave nodded before he stood up again. It still seemed like something was bothering him.

I started to leave, but decided to ask so I stopped at the door and turned around. "Dave, are you okay?"

He blinked at me for a moment. He seemed to be trying to put something into words. "I just wonder if I'm doing myself any favors is all."

That didn't make sense to me. "I can listen, you know… and keep a secret. But I understand if it's something you'd rather not talk about."

He sighed and closed his eyes for a minute. When he opened them, they seemed to have regained their humor. "It's nothing, really. I promise not to be weird tomorrow. Now let's get out of here so you can get some sleep."

"Don't make promises you can't keep," I teased.

He laughed and gently pushed me out of his office. We walked out together and he waved from his car as I drove off in mine.

I thought I loved working at the restaurant when I was simply popping in and out of it. Getting to stay there hours at a time was even more fun. Of course I had to deal with more of "the public" so there were occasional hassles. I had to ask one couple to leave after repeatedly asking them to stop making out at the table. A rowdy group of guys thought it was hilarious to dump several containers worth of parmesan under their booth and then track it out the front door. And I did get a fair amount of comments about the "Enjoy!" on the back of my shirt. Most of those were pretty harmless. One group of guys kept coming up with excuses to call me to their table so they could snicker at enjoying me walk away. When I brought the check, Brandon was at the table. I don't know what he said to them, but I ended up with a sincere-sounding apology for wasting my time and a nice tip.

Overall customers were pretty polite though. It was a nice change to be around long enough to hear exclamations of how good the pizza was. More than anything, I enjoyed my teams. I tried to keep my loyalty even, mostly for appearance's sake. Amy seemed to have gotten over her crush, but she was not the only one who was obviously one-sided.

My apartment plan worked out and I worked at Pizza Heaven through the summer and settled into a regular schedule during my final year of school. That's when the last hour of each night became my favorite time of day. Delivery orders were pretty strong until close, but the dining room got quiet at the end. Josh had graduated and moved on and either Connor or Julie helped Dave in the kitchen. Whoever was on left at nine. Drivers came in only long enough to pick up orders and Brandon hung out in the office. I usually found excuses to stay in the kitchen with Dave if it wasn't obvious where my help was needed and then it would be just the two of us. He had shown me most of his secrets so I could put together pizzas or answer the phone.

"What are you eating?" Dave asked me one night.

I knew he was about to give me a hard time because he could see that I was using a fork to eat shredded cheese off a plate. "Cheese," I told him.

"There's a perfectly good pizza right there." He pointed to the usual spot. There was about a third of a pizza remaining.

"I had two slices already. I just wanted a small snack."

"I cannot believe you're insulting my cooking by eating that in front of me."

114

"Your ego is so fragile that you're insulted by cheese?"

"It wasn't the cheese who claimed to be on my team only about five minutes ago."

"You don't believe I'm on your team? Now I'm the one who's insulted."

"You're not insulted. I know you like Brandon better."

"You don't believe I'm insulted either. Now you've done it." I closed my eyes and prepared to unleash my not-so-secret weapon. Dave knew what I was doing.

"No! You can't do the crying thing. That's not fighting fair."

I was trying so hard not to laugh that I could only manage to make my eyes sort of moist. "You brought this on yourself," I insisted anyway.

Dave let out a groan of frustration before he picked up a plate. I watched as he arranged a ring of pepperoni and olives, my two favorite toppings, and piled cheese in the center. He handed it to me and said, "Here. No tears allowed."

"Wow, Dave, this might be the most impressive thing you've ever made for me."

He rolled his eyes. "You really know how to hurt a guy, don't you?"

"Okay, we all know your pizza is amazing. In fact, I'm surprised your head isn't as big as this kitchen with how often you hear it."

"It's not like I can take credit for the recipe. It was my great-grandmother's and for all I know she got it off a jar." It wasn't fake humility.

"I'm sure it was her creation, or at least someone in the family. I don't think they had jars back then."

"Is that a crack about my age?"

I laughed, but only because I hadn't meant that at all. Dave had recently turned 28 and was fretting about "knocking on 30." I would have thought the fact that Julie, who was only 18, looked at him as though he was more delicious than his cooking might have kept him from feeling old. But I still hadn't meant a reference to his age. "I only meant," I began to clarify, "that I thought everything was made from scratch in those days and not that you're so old your great-grandmother must predate glass. Why are you so sensitive tonight?"

Dave looked thoughtful for a moment, as though maybe I was right about him being sensitive. I was distracted by a phone order and never found out if he came up with a reason.

Most times he was not so sensitive. He gave as good as he got and the mood stayed playful. Occasionally, however, those quiet last hours took a more serious turn.

I locked the front door behind the person who had been manning it. "All done up front," I said as I returned to the kitchen.

"You don't have to wait for Aaron with me."

"If I leave now, there won't be anyone to walk me out. Besides, I know you love my company."

Dave grinned at me. I thought I might be standing too close to the oven. It stayed hot for a while after it was turned off for the night. "I'm not the one who comes up with excuses to stay in the kitchen."

"You know I only do that for your sake." I plopped myself on the stool next to him. "So is there anything new with you?"

"You see me five times a week. I think you'd know."

"Hmm... you must have something interesting to talk about."

"Oh, you know what? I heard from Lance today. Just a brief email, but it sounded like he was doing pretty well. He's thinking of moving to Maine."

I nodded. "I'm glad he's happy."

"You don't have any regrets there, do you? I mean, I know it's none of my business. I just want to know if I'm an idiot for bringing him up."

"Well, you are an idiot..."

Dave smiled appreciatively. He knew he opened himself up to that one.

"However," I continued, "no, I don't. I regret that he got hurt, but I don't regret ending it. We just weren't going to work out long term."

"Did you know it wasn't right before he proposed?"

"Before he what?!"

"Oh my gosh! He didn't? Oh, no... He showed me the ring and I just assumed that was when..."

Both of my hands were over my mouth and I didn't remember putting them there. I would have preferred to go the rest of my life without knowing that the heart I broke was even more committed to me than I had realized. But I couldn't change that. Dave was still apologizing and I thought I should try to minimize the damage that I could control.

117

"… didn't have any idea that you hadn't said 'no.' I'm so sorry. Please forgive me for being the biggest idiot ever."

"Dave, stop. It was an honest mistake and other than a moment of surprise it doesn't really make a difference." His hand was resting on the counter beside us and I patted it with mine. I intended it as a comforting gesture, but had to pull back quickly. A weird jolt of electricity shot through my arm and made me temporarily forget, as seemed to be happening a lot lately, that this was a man toward whom I had sisterly feelings. My tingling nerves made me want to keep talking. "You asked if I knew before… before the end. I think I didn't want to know. He always made me feel so important. I felt like there was someone other than my parents who would do anything for me and that was hard to give up even after I knew I wasn't going to feel the same way about him."

Dave nodded understandingly so I guess I was making sense.

"It makes me sound like a terrible person, doesn't it?"

"No, it doesn't. We can't help who we fall in love with or who we don't fall in love with. Only what we do about it. I think you handled it the best you could."

I shook my head. "If I'm being totally honest, and this will make you think less of me, I don't think it was my lack of return feelings that made me call it quits. I might have strung him along longer if it hadn't been for other stuff. That is, if he didn't force the issue with a ring."

Dave winced. I felt a pang for bringing up his accidental revelation. Then he asked, "What other stuff?"

118

"We talked about the future and it became clear that his plans didn't mesh with mine."

"How so?"

"He was leaning toward one kid, two at most. I feel like I kind of missed out on something by having no siblings. I'm not talking about a boatload of children, but I think I'd like three or four."

Dave smiled. "There are some things you're lucky you missed out on. Sometimes I wonder how all of us made it to adulthood."

There were five kids in Dave's family, four of them boys, and he was the baby. I had heard more than a few stories. One of the scariest was the time when he was 12 when he broke his arm after two of his brothers convinced him to "surf" down a flight of stairs on a plastic sled. They were indoor stairs with a wall at the bottom.

"Lance also thought it would be cool to move to a new city every few years to see new places. I don't see anything wrong with this city right here so I wouldn't want to move without a really good reason. What some people call boring, I call stable."

"Stable is good."

I was staring at the floor by this time and feeling unusually self-conscious. "Um, I think it's your turn now."

"My turn for what?"

"I don't know. I feel like I'm all soul-baring here or something and I feel… like…" I stopped and bit my lip. I didn't know how to explain the uncomfortable feeling that I might have shared too much. And I really had no idea why I thought asking him to do the same would make me feel better.

"What do you want to know?"

"I don't know. I... have *you* ever broken anyone's heart?"

"Not that I'm aware of."

I suspected he'd dented a few without knowing it. Not returning a crush was different though. "What about yours. No past stomping?"

He shook his head. "Not yet. I'm afraid it's, well, only a matter of time."

"That's a strange thing to say. You always seem like an optimist."

"Well, you don't have all the facts."

"Oh! So there's someone..."

"I'm not going to talk about that. Let's just say that I don't yet have any relationship battle scars and then you pick a different way for me to bare my soul, as you put it."

I lowered my eyes so Dave couldn't see how completely thrown I was by his admission. I had witnessed a few crushes at Pizza Heaven. It was delusional for me to assume Brandon or Dave would never notice anyone, especially since they spent more time at the restaurant than anyone else. Dave interrupted my thoughts.

"You're trying to think of a way to make me talk, aren't you? Just pick a new topic."

I laughed. "That's not what I was thinking, but okay, new topic. What about... well, what about your relationship with Brandon? Did you ever think that going into business together might jeopardize your friendship?"

"No."

"Never?"

"No. I thought that if we could survive his parents' death, then we could survive inventory squabbles."

"Right. I feel bad that I sometimes forget what he's been through. He's always so happy now."

"He is. He... it took a while."

"I'm sure it would. I don't even want to think about what I'd do."

Dave took a heavy breath and let it out slowly. "All right. I'm going to tell you something I've never told anyone and then we're going to be even."

I nodded, a little afraid of getting what I asked for.

"When Brandon's parents died, it was... I'm not going to pretend I was going through anything like what Brandon was, but I had known them my whole life, too. It was shocking and I was only 18 so it was a lot to deal with. The worst part was that I didn't know how to help Brandon. He was in a dark place for a long time. He pushed everyone away, got angry with me over anything, you know, just always looking for reasons to pick a fight. I tried to take it because I knew he was hurting, but... I yelled back a lot of times. Once, things got really ugly and I said... I told him that if he kept being a jerk to everyone that he wouldn't only be without parents, he'd also be without friends. That's when he hit me."

"Like really hit you?"

"Like I had a black eye for a week."

"Wow."

"Yeah. It was the only time either of us... I mean, we wrestled around some when we were kids..."

121

"And last week."

A faint smile broke through. I was glad to see I wasn't bringing him too far down. "And I guess we still do, but never... it's always in jest, you know. We didn't talk for a few weeks after that, but eventually... I totally deserved the smackdown so we both apologized and things improved. Slowly. It was months before his old self started to return."

"And you never even told your parents?"

Dave shook his head.

"Didn't people wonder where you got the shiner?"

"I told everyone that I walked into a wall."

"People believed that?"

"These were mostly people who knew how I broke my arm." He smiled wryly at me and I felt very strange. As though I was experiencing something completely new. But I had talked about private things with Lance and told my parents some of the same things about our breakup that Dave now knew. I couldn't figure out why this time felt unique. I rubbed my sweaty hands on my thighs hoping he didn't notice what he was doing to me. I happened to glance at the clock.

"Oh my goodness. It's after 10:30. Do you think we should be worried about Aaron?"

Dave surprised me by bursting into laughter. "Oh, no," he said. "I forgot. Oh... Aaron's coming in tomorrow so I told him he could go straight home after his last delivery. Don't be mad, but we're sitting here waiting for someone who isn't coming back."

I laughed because I was far from angry. I was actually kind of disappointed because I didn't want to leave and now we had nothing keeping us there. Dave knew that as well as I did. He got up and grabbed our coats. He handed mine to me without saying anything. When we went to the parking lot a minute later, he touched the small of my back lightly as though guiding me through the door. I think he had done that other times without my paying it any attention. That night I remembered his earlier words about not being able to help who we fall in love with. I knew that was true. If it wasn't true, I would not have let myself fall for a guy who had all but admitted he was in love with someone else.

It turned out that Dave and I were not the only ones having a serious talk that night. Brandon came in the next day and announced his engagement. That was cause for celebration. Dave baked a cake. I don't know how he managed that in a pizza oven, but it was so good. It was a little crispy on the edges and we ate it warm with gooey frosting.

Julie said, "This is too good not to add to the menu."

Dave shook his head, as usual. Sometimes he made things other than pizza just for the team and someone always suggested it be added to the menu. He and Brandon held firm to the idea that you don't fix what isn't broken. And Dave didn't want to make more work for himself.

"People would pay good money for this," I added.

"We don't have a dessert menu and we are not going to."

"You have to at least make this for us again. Now that I know you make cake I'm going to be very sad if I have to wait 'til someone else gets engaged to have some."

Dave smiled. "I might be talked into making some again for anyone who's on my team."

Everyone in the room, including Brandon, said, "Team Dave!"

I watched Dave closely for weeks after that, trying to figure out if the person he thought would break his heart worked with us. His eyes never followed anyone out of the kitchen. If it was someone at Pizza Heaven, he was guarding it very well. And if she was somewhere else, there probably wasn't anything I could do about that either.

He made a few more cakes for the team. Even though we had to share them with whomever was working, I felt like he was doing it for me. We talked about a lot of things over those cakes, usually frivolous things with lots of teasing. We never talked about the fact that I was about to graduate though. I felt like it was assumed that I would leave for a job with numbers once I had that degree. Other employees who graduated looked for jobs in their fields. I wanted Dave to ask what my plans were. I wanted him to care. I wanted him to miss me more than he missed everyone else who left. But he never said anything.

Jake graduated with me. He was going to grad school in Texas and we all knew that. Julie was going home for the summer and asked if I would still be there when she returned. I shrugged. That shrug was as close as I got to discussing my career plans, or lack thereof, with anyone at work until a few weeks into the summer.

"Shall we have dessert tonight?" Dave asked me.

"I thought that was becoming a Friday thing."

"Yeah, well, Brandon found out that we've been having cake on his night off." Brandon emerged from the office just then and Dave added, "Speak of the devil," under his breath.

"Guys, you gotta help me with my homework."

"Homework? And here I thought you were in there making sure we don't run out of food."

"Relax, Kitchen Master, I ordered all your precious ingredients first. Now tell me how to answer this."

Brandon was holding a purple booklet with a pair of rings on the cover. He and his fiancée were taking a marriage prep class.

"We're not going to help you," Dave said. "You're supposed to answer those questions by yourself."

"No, the point is for me to answer without Kate so we can compare answers later."

"I'm pretty sure that's not the point," Dave insisted.

"Fine. I don't need you anyway. Kara will help me."

"Well," I said, "I am kind of curious now."

"Great. This question wants to know how we will make decisions together. If I put 'talk about it' does that sound glib? I can't think of any other ways to make a decision."

I shrugged. "That sounds fine."

Brandon nodded. "Okay. Here's one that says, 'What do you think might be your biggest weakness as a parent?' Obviously, I don't have any weaknesses so…" He smirked over the top of the booklet. I thought he was more serious than he was letting on.

"If you really want my opinion," I started. Brandon nodded eagerly so I kept going. "I think you might be more of a softie than you realize. You may have to make sure you aren't wrapped too tightly around anyone's finger."

Brandon looked thoughtful for a moment. Then he turned to Dave and said, "She's pretty smart. No wonder we keep her around."

Dave looked at me with a mix of admiration and annoyance. His expression did something funny to my stomach. "Why are you helping him," he asked.

"I don't know. You hired me to be helpful, right?"

"This is not in your job description."

"All right," Brandon said. "I'll leave now, but I'm taking Kara with me." He hooked his arm through mine and led me back toward the office. He called back to Dave over his shoulder. "Don't worry, I won't try to get her to help me anymore. We're just going to talk about you for a while."

I peeked behind us and saw Dave rolling his eyes. Brandon brought us into the office and asked me to have a seat. He took the other chair and looked at me. "I'm curious," he said, "whether or not you're looking for a full time job now that you're done with school."

The question surprised me. I really thought he was going to ask me more about his "homework." "I…"

"Wait! Don't think we're trying to get rid of you or anything. I mean, if we did Employee of the Month - it'd be you all the time. But here's the thing… we can add lunch Tuesday and Thursday to bring you up to 40 hours if you're interested. On the other hand, not everyone loves pizza as much as me and Dave so if you're looking for something else… honestly, that might make things easier… but we're really not trying to get rid of you."

Easier? Did Brandon know!? Was he trying to suggest that if there was a guy I was pining away for it might be easier not to spend so many hours a week standing next to him? That might have been some sound brotherly advice. And Brandon was still like a brother to me. I'd miss him if I left, too. How could I visit only on Dave's night off without…? There was nothing easy about this. Brandon was sitting there waiting for me to answer. I was going to ignore the easier part and play dumb. "Well, I am going to have to start paying off student loans soon so I wouldn't say no to more hours."

Brandon nodded. "Okay. Next week we'll see more of you. Now…" He reached for that purple booklet again. "I have to get back to work so if you're not going to help, you might as well go back to the kitchen and make Dave happy."

I couldn't get that conversation with Brandon out of my head. I didn't want to leave and I didn't want to stay. Not the way things were. I was starting to think about letting Dave make the decision for me. If I could somehow work up the courage to tell him how I felt about him it would probably be awkward and terrible, but at least I'd know what I had to do.

I made it almost through the summer before I decided to say something. I was helping him wash some pans when I said. "I don't know what I'm doing."

He gave me a funny look. "How many times have you washed that pan without knowing how?"

I pulled my hand out of the sink and flicked soapy water at him. "I'm not talking about the pan."

"Then what are you talking about?"

I handed him the pan to rinse and we both dried our hands before I said anything else. Dave looked like he was about to ask again what I was talking about.

"It's 10 o'clock. I should lock the front so Sam can go home."

He nodded. He hadn't moved when I returned. He was waiting for me with a puzzled look on his face.

"I guess I should have said that I don't know what I'm *going* to do."

"About what?"

"About... I don't have a plan anymore."

Dave took a few steps closer to me. He was starting to go from puzzled to concerned. I wondered if perhaps he thought I was losing my mind. "What kind of plan?"

"I guess... my life."

"I'm sorry. I still don't know what you mean."

"When I started, I thought I'd work here only during college. I thought I'd eventually move on to... why else study accounting, right? But now I can't imagine working anywhere but here." I shook my head. The reason I didn't want to leave could have been inserted right there. But I was so nervous I started to feel like I might cry, really cry, so I took a breath to steady myself.

128

"There's no rush, we aren't going to kick you to the curb just because you have a degree."

"I know. I just thought you'd be expecting me to leave and it might be awkward if I kept hanging around and you didn't know it was because I *wanted* to be here. It seems like everyone else leaves when they graduate and I can't tell you why I don't want to leave. I tried and I can't." I was such a coward. Maybe I needed to write a note. That's what cowards did.

Dave was staring at me. He didn't say anything for a long minute. I knew I was turning red and I sort of wished I had a nice, comfortable hole to crawl into.

"You could do our books," he said suddenly.

"What?"

"I'd have to talk to Brandon, but that's his least favorite part anyway. I don't know why I didn't think of this before." He seemed to be talking and thinking at the same time. "What if we did that? It wouldn't be enough for a full time job, but you could fill the extra hours with, you know, pizza stuff. Everyone could be happy because there would be numbers involved and you'd still be working here. You don't have to leave."

I was smiling with overflowing relief. I didn't care what my plan was anymore. I only knew that Dave cared what my plan was. "Wow," I said. "You sound almost as desperate to keep me here as I am to stay."

He whispered one word, I think it was "more," before he closed the gap between us with one step and was kissing me with such urgency that I couldn't breathe or even quite register what was

129

happening. I was aware of clutching fistfuls of the front of his shirt. I didn't think my heart could beat any faster when we heard the back door open.

Dave jumped backward and looked more flustered than I had ever seen anyone. He muttered, "I'm so sorry," and then called out, "Hey, Aaron… walk Kara out, will you? I just have a bit of paperwork tonight."

"Sure thing, boss," came the reply from around the corner. "Team Dave did awesome in tips tonight, by the way."

Dave shook his head and practically ran to his office and closed the door. That door was never closed. I tried to get outside without Aaron seeing my face. He was conveniently oblivious. I made it all the way back to my apartment before the tears came. Hot, heavy tears that I couldn't control and didn't know if I'd ever be able to stop.

I called in sick the next day. I was very glad that Brandon answered the phone. In almost three years, I had never called in sick and it was humiliating that Dave would know why. He regretted kissing me. That was the only reason the apology made sense. I had never regretted anything less and that was why I wasn't ready to see him.

I called in sick again on Sunday. On Monday, I decided that three days was enough time to pick up the pieces of my pride, slap a band-aid on my heart and wipe the confounded expression off my face. Dave was normal to everyone else all day. He said only work-related things to me and never once made eye contact. The distance helped me act normally toward everyone else as well. I was grateful that he was at least helping me save face. But I was determined that I would get him alone eventually. Painful as it might be, I wanted him to explain his regrets and why he had kissed me in the first place if he was just going to take it back. Had he just gotten caught up in a moment? Was there any way that I could pretend I had, too?

Dave seemed just as determined to avoid me. Even during that typically quiet last hour of the day, he pretended to put every ounce of concentration into the work we both knew he could do in his sleep. I tried to talk to him once and he shook his head and said, "Not now."

It was probably best to wait until the end of the shift anyway. I wasn't sure I could keep my composure and that would be the end of any face-saving. Brandon left just before ten and then I said goodnight to a few customers who had to be reminded that we were closing. I locked the door behind them. Jake had just come back when I went into the kitchen. I heard him asking Dave if there was anything left to go out.

"No, Aaron just grabbed the last two. You're free to go."

Jake nodded. "Well, I think I'm off for a while so you guys have a good week."

"'Night, Jake," I said.

Dave waved at him. It was extremely quiet in the seconds after the door closed behind Jake. Dave turned to me, "Aaron should be back in no more than ten minutes. He can walk you out. Please wait for him." He walked into the office. I tried to stop him and

131

he practically closed the door in my face. Did he think making me angry was going to improve the tension?

I waited for Aaron by the back door even though I had no intention of leaving with him. He came in shortly and put his car magnet and pizza bag away. "How was your night?" I asked him.

"Not too bad really. Are you done, too?"

"Actually, no. I was slacking and haven't gotten around to wiping down the menus yet. But Dave's almost done. I'll walk out with him."

"All right. See you tomorrow then."

I nodded and waved. I went around to Dave's office. The back door was loud so I knew he heard it. I don't think it took ten seconds for him to come out. He froze when he saw me.

"I'm not leaving until you talk to me. I kind of thought we could talk about anything."

"We... I don't know what to say other than I'm sorry." He just stood there refusing to look at me. I didn't want him to be sorry. And I felt like I was hurting him simply by being there, which was even worse.

"Do you want me to quit?"

"No!" Dave seemed as surprised by his anger as I was. He softened. "No, I don't want you to quit. I know how much you love working here. I've been trying for so long to avoid putting you in a situation where you felt like..." He ran his hands through his hair and slumped onto a nearby stool. "I can't believe you're talking about quitting. I let my guard down for a second and ruin everything."

132

"I'm not talking about quitting. I'm asking you what you want. I thought I was confused before and then… what happened?"

"You were there."

"That doesn't mean I know what happened. Can you explain it to me as though I wasn't there?"

He put his head in his hands. I'd like to say I waited patiently. His hesitation seemed to last forever though. I kept using my sleeve in a hopeless attempt to keep my face dry in case he looked up. He didn't. He eventually talked to the floor. "I can't explain it. All I know is I couldn't figure out why you suddenly thought you might lose your job and I wanted to reassure you. I thought I was going to just give you a quick hug and that somehow turned into something about a million times more inappropriate."

Inappropriate? Now I was beginning to understand why Dave had apologized. He had evidently missed the part where I kissed him back. I decided to be offended by that later since other, more important, things were also becoming clearer. "You meant me, didn't you?"

His mumbled answer was still aimed at the floor. "I don't know what you're talking about."

"Do you remember that night a few months ago when we were waiting for Aaron and he wasn't coming?"

"Of course."

"I asked if you had ever had your heart broken and you said you thought it was only a matter of time. You meant me, didn't you?"

Dave finally looked at me. "Does that help? I'd think it would make you even more uncomfortable to know how much… that I…

133

that it wasn't a fleeting impulse, but... is there anything I can do that *would* help?"

"Pretend I'm on Brandon's team."

"What?"

"Stop thinking about me as your employee because that's not what happened. I didn't tell my boss that I wanted to keep my job. At least... I was trying to tell *you* that I wanted to stay here. With you. I was trying to tell you that I... I love you."

Dave's expression changed from miserable to confused to a fairly happy normal while the atmosphere around us went through a similar transformation. It was a different, better normal. I couldn't think of anything to say that might improve it so I stood there quietly wondering how Dave would break the silence.

"Let me get this straight," he said. "Even though I am technically your employer, you are *not* freaked out by what happened?"

"Um, not the good part."

Those long lashes covered his eyes for a moment while he tried not to smile. He looked flattered and embarrassed at the same time. It was very cute. "Kara?" he asked.

"Yes."

"Would you like to go to Brandon's wedding with me?"

"You already know I'm going to be there."

"Yeah, but I'd like it if you went with me. I want to make sure I can find you."

"What do you mean?"

"How will I recognize you without your Pizza Heaven shirt?"

134

"You're not gonna wear yours?"

He stopped laughing and looked at me more seriously. "Please say that I can take you."

"Okay. And I'll add that I'm really looking forward to it."

"I should warn you though. If you go to a wedding with me I'll probably start to get ideas."

"Ideas?" Was he talking about what I thought he was talking about?

"I'm not saying I'd ask the next day or anything. It's just... Considering my age and all, I can't be expected to wait forever. And I know you're trying to figure some things out so I hoped you'd factor my intentions into any decisions you're making."

"Okay." I was having a little trouble wrapping my head around those intentions. But in a good way.

Dave stood and asked, "Shall we call it a night?"

"Do we have to?"

"No. But to be honest, I haven't slept much recently."

"Believe me when I say I understand. Don't ever apologize for kissing me again."

There was a mischievous twinkle in his eyes as he grinned at me. "Do you mean that?"

The look he was giving me nearly melted me into a puddle on the floor. Since I couldn't seem to find my voice, I simply nodded.

He moved closer and wrapped his arms around my waist. I couldn't lift my eyes past the logo on his shirt because I was suddenly very nervous. There had been no time to anticipate the first kiss and he seemed intent on making up for that. Or maybe he was nervous, too. He was so close I could smell the pizza scent on his shirt. It was familiar and encouraging.

When I looked up he said, "I love you, too," before his lips finally touched mine. The kiss was gentler than the first time yet still more enthusiastic than I expected. And I thought the pizza oven was hot.

Did you enjoy *Meet Cute*?

Why not check out a full length romantic comedy?

The 4th Floor Lounge (2012)

Where does an extreme introvert draw the line between being lonely and being left alone? One quirky college student is looking for the answer in the 4th floor lounge.

Her goals are simple: make one or two good friends and avoid talking to everyone else. Achieving those goals will not be easy for this gorgeous yet socially awkward heroine. She's constantly approached by guys who are not interested in friendship. And when she finally forms some solid bonds it's her own romantic feelings that get in the way.

Weathering Evan (2012)

Tammy Janeway is having some issues. Evan Knightly is at the root of all of them. Of course it's not his fault that she has a massive crush on him. But she can't even be sure he deserves her adoration. One minute he's undeniably sweet and charming, the next he acts like a creep.

Tammy is tired of feeling like a nervous teenager in her professional life. She knows she's making a fool of herself in front of the coworker who is already dating Evan. She knows she can't stop thinking about him and she knows she wants to. But the one thing she doesn't know just might be the key to finding a fresh start.

Tightening the Knot (2009)

Meredith Donnor is no longer searching for the man of her dreams. She married him six years earlier. But her romantic life has gotten off track. To avoid an uncomfortable subject, she and Greg are barely speaking - distractions at work, where Meredith teaches first grade, are not helping - and Meredith's penchant for over-thinking generates more anxiety than answers. She becomes increasingly frustrated as her hints to restart communication go unnoticed and Greg's return gesture comes with its own set of problems.

When they finally escape to the "Tightening the Knot" marriage seminar, they believe there is more to laugh at than benefit from. But could humor provide the breakthrough this humorless situation needs?

Dear Jane Letters (2007)

Dear Jane Letters is a light-hearted look into the life of Raina Lane, author of a local advice column titled Dear Jane. Raina has a close family who loves and entertains her at every encounter. She lives with her best friend, Vicki, who is about to get married and is anxious to see Raina paired up as well. She looks for romance between Raina and just about anyone with whom they come into contact, including a blind date and the old friend who has recently reentered Raina's life.

Despite her roommate's constant vigilance, when Raina does find love, it still catches her by surprise.